Cold Wind
A Novel by Ray Derby

Cold Wind

INTRODUCTION

For many years I have been asked by those who read my novel 'The Shadow Government' if I would consider writing a sequel to it. My answer to most was no. I had no desire to do so. Now some sixteen years later I have done what I said I would not do, written a sequel to 'The Shadow Government'.

I hope you enjoy it.

Ray Derby

COLD WIND

Chapter 1

June 2040

The White House bunker built after the assault on the nation in 2019, was small and cramped but even now, some twenty years later, it contained the most sophisticated communications and electronics systems in the world. On a normal day for eighteen hours, it was a hub of activity. The night shift is what the staff called the graveyard shift. They used this shift to maintain or upgrade the systems. Therefore, between 10 p.m. and 4 a.m. every day, unless a crisis was brewing or on-going, the bunker was quiet. This suited Wendy just fine.

Lying on one of the bunks that folded up against the wall like on a ship when not in use, she could feel the thin mattress against her slim body. She thought, all the comforts of home and smiled in the dim darkness. She could hear the faint hum of the communication and electronic systems as the sound circulated throughout the bunker and it seemed as if they were just waiting for something to happen...anything so that they could spring to life.

She had hoped to catch a few hours of sleep but like many other nights, she knew it was not to be and finally slid out of the bunk. She wondered if she could ever get over the nightmares of seeing the streets of Washington, DC littered with the thousands of dead bodies and the weeks it took to recover the bodies so they could bury them at sea. She knew the answer...*never!*

When the enemy struck, using a deadly biological agent, the United States was totally unprepared for a crisis of that magnitude. It had taken years for the country to recover from its effects.

They planned and executed the attack well. Millions of Americans across the country had lost their lives and it had been only luck and the insight of a few individuals that had prevented a total collapse of the nation. It was only at the end of the attack on the country that she became involved with those heroes who defended the country and became a part of that group and participated in its rebirth.

Wendy dressed, poured a cup of coffee from the pot in the small galley, pitch black and steaming hot, then slowly moved over to a chair around the conference table and sat down. As she looked around the room, the blank TV screens seem to glare back at her and she thought, Christ, how long have I been coming here, but again, she knew the answer. She had helped build the bunker some twenty years ago and now it was almost like a second home to her. With her hands cupped around the coffee mug, she leaned back and let her mind drift back to that late-summer day when she and a small group of Marines waited on the tarmac at Andrews Air Force Base for the president to arrive. It seemed like yesterday, yet some twenty years had elapsed.

She, like the others in her group had watched the three executive jet aircrafts circle the base and then one by one land and taxi up to the base operations building. A presidential limousine was parked a few hundred feet away and the Secret Service detail stood beside it. Her small squad was not there to protect the new president but would have if called to do so. Each Marine carried a rifle and all of them were proficient in its use. They were part of an honor guard.

She remembered thinking, I hope we have an opportunity to at least catch a glimpse of her before she gets in the limo. Even now, what happened next still gave her goose bumps when she thought about it. As the president walked down the steps of the aircraft, the lieutenant brought the squad to attention and then from the corner of her eye could see her start to walk to the limousine then suddenly she stopped and turned in the direction of the honor guard. At first Wendy was not sure what she was going to do, and then she watched as the president walked toward her group.

What happened next changed her life forever. Before she knew it, Bea Singleton the new president of the United States was standing before her and what happened then became a legend within the Marine Corps.

"What is your name?" the president asked.

"Lance Corporal Darwin, Sir, I mean Madam President," she replied.

The president had smiled. "All right, Lance Corporal Darwin, what is your first name?"

"It's Wendy, Ma'am."

"All right, Wendy, you may call me Bea."

Standing rigidly at attention she had replied, "I'm sorry, Ma'am, I cannot do that. You are the president of the United States and my commander-in-chief."

This comment startled the president for a moment but then she asked, "What branch of the military are you in, Wendy?" Dressed in battle fatigues, it would have taken a military person to know.

"The US Marines," she had replied.

"And how old are you, Wendy?"

"I'm twenty-six, Ma'am." The next question had again caught Wendy off guard and she wondered where all this was going.

The president asked, "Have you ever been in combat?"

She answered, "Yes, Ma'am." Which again startled the president.

Then the president said, "All right, Lance Corporal Darwin, as your commander in chief I am hereby reassigning you as my aide-de-camp and, and you will come with me."

With her mind in turmoil Wendy turned to the young lieutenant who headed the detail, "Sir, permission to be relieved of duty at the request of the president of the United States."

The lieutenant standing ramrod straight turned and faced her, "Permission granted."

Only then did she turn and walk with the president to the limo.

That one request; permission to be relieved of duty by the president of the United States was a legend throughout the Corps, and she knew those words would stay with her for the rest of her life.

****

Wendy sensed rather than saw that someone had entered the room. Then she heard the voice, "Ma'am, you have a priority call in the situation room."

Lieutenant General Wendy Darwin stood and wondered now what, as she left the room.

Chapter 2

The man had been driving for several hours and he was tired but he kept his guard up. He had made it a point to move in random patterns as he traveled through the large cities and he drove straight through the small towns in order not to draw attention to the car or himself. He was positive he was not followed today but, nothing was a sure thing. Some thirty minutes ago he had seen a blue Ford sedan move in behind him for some twenty miles before it had turned into a lane that went to a two-story farmhouse. As soon as he reached the crest of a small hill, he moved to the side of the road and parked. Although it was almost dusk, he could see there was no traffic on the secondary road. All he could see in either direction was rows of corn some three feet high. He quickly moved back to the crest of the hill and with a pair of high-powered binoculars he crouched alongside the road and trained them on the farmhouse. He breathed a little easier as he saw a man in what appeared to be farm clothing and a woman slowly walk toward the front porch of the house.

He waited until both had entered the house and only then did he breathe a sigh of relief and head back to his car. He might be overreacting but he knew he could not take any chances. He must complete his mission even if it cost him his life. He pulled the car back onto the road and continued his journey.

As the man and woman entered the farmhouse, they joined several individuals who were closely watching a TV screen. One of the men stood and they noted the jacket he wore with the Federal Bureau of Investigation (FBI) logo patch.

The man dressed as a farmer stated, "Well, I hope that worked, but I still think it was a risky thing to do."

The FBI agent replied, "We need to keep pressing him and maybe just maybe he will make a mistake. If he is only a courier, it's vital we find out who his contacts are. If he is only a little fish, he might just take us to the bigger ones. He did take the bait and stopped to check to see if you were following him or just a farmer and his wife returning home. He appears to have bought it and now is continuing to his destination, wherever that may be."

The woman asked, "Is the satellite still on him?"

"Yes," the agent replied, "but we will lose it within the next two hours and ten minutes. So, let's hope he will reach his journey's end before then or we may be screwed."

Chapter 3

Wendy replaced the secure phone in its cradle and turned to the duty officer. "Have a copy of that conversation sent to the president's chief of staff so it can be included in the daily situation briefing."

"Yes, ma'am," the officer replied and then asked, "are there any other recipients?"

"No," Wendy replied and left the room.

Now some three hours later she slowly drove her car along the narrow roads surrounded by the white crosses and monuments. Arlington National Cemetery was still quiet but she knew it would not be long before people would be here by the thousands to pay homage to those who had perished defending the country. After the assault on the nation in 2019 it had become even more revered as a holy place. She parked the car on the small rise and walked up the gentle slope until she reached her destination.

Off to the side of the burial plot stood a single Marine facing the tombstones. He remained at parade rest with his legs spread apart and his hands behind his back. She knew he would not move if she or anyone else was in that area. Like the tomb of the unknown soldier, this solitary Marine in full dress uniform and others like him stood guard over this hallowed ground twenty-four hours a day, seven days a week. The only real difference between the two memorials was the fact that only the Marine Corps provided the honor guard detail here and it was the most sought-after assignment in the Corps. She knew he would keep that stance until she left. God, she again thought how many years have I been coming here? Of course, she knew that answer as well, on this warm June day in 2040. Some twenty-one years had passed.

She gazed at the five headstones and the memories flooded back as if it were yesterday. And like all the other times, the sadness was tempered with pride at having known three of these people. All the headstones were made of white marble with the name at the top of the stone, then a small description and finally the dates they were born and died. As she looked at the first headstone the words came into focus.

Robert L. Hardy

The 45th President of the United States. He conceived and secretly funded the Blue Light Project to ensure our country would remain free.

Douglas M. McKay

Chairman of the Joint Chiefs of Staff. He served his country with honor and his memory lives on in the history of the Blue Light facilities.

As she glanced at the third headstone, the sadness seeped over her. When she first met this individual, her life had changed forever.

Beatrice A. Singleton

The 46th and first woman President of the United States. She is credited with the rebuilding of our country and became the most distinguished world leader in history.

The next headstone took the sadness away because this man also had been her mentor and friend for many years.

Nathan E. Sems

The 47th President of the United States. He is credited for completing the Blue Light project and preserving those facilities as part of our national monuments in honor of those who survived and rebuilt our country.

Finally, she looked at the last monument and a fierce pride surged over her. This gravesite would have seemed out of place being next to three presidents except for one thing. At the top of this white marble headstone not one but two

Congressional Medals of Honor were engraved into the granite. The simple description read:

<u>Norman C. Shepard</u>

Lieutenant Colonel U.S. Marine Corps. He gave his life so our country might live.

Although she had never met Lieutenant Colonel Norm Shepard, she had heard firsthand on many occasions how Presidents Singleton and Sems thought of his courage and duty to his country. Wendy was aware, as most Americans were not, that it was he who saved President Singleton at the cost of his own life.

She turned and looked at the Marine standing at parade rest and with that fierce pride still coursing through her she came to attention like she had done many times before and saluted the guard. What happened next astounded her. The guard suddenly came to ridged attention and slowly as if in slow motion raised his right arm and returned the salute. Never in all the time she had been coming here had that happened. The pride surged through her again and she dropped the salute, turned and walked to her car. As she opened her car door, she once more glanced up at the grave site. The lone sentry was still standing at attention holding the salute.

What General Darwin did not know was that for years those in the Marine Corps, and especially those men and women who had volunteered to man that post, were keenly aware that she always saluted not the heroes lying in state, but the lone guard who stood watch over them. The protocol established at the creation of the honor guard dictated that the guard would stand at parade rest always while guarding the site. There were no exceptions.

Wendy would have been surprised at how fiercely that battle had waged over the years for the right to return her salute. She, like every other individual, made friends and enemies as they moved along the career ladder, and for whatever the reason no change in the guards' protocols had ever been authorized.

Staff Sergeant Dale Dotson watched as General Darwin left and only then slowly dropped the salute and returned to parade rest. He knew a precedence had been set and his brothers and sisters in uniform would make sure it stayed that way. He also knew his sixteen-year career with the Marine Corps was over but he had no regrets at what he had done. He, like most military and civilians, knew that General Darwin had from the start helped rebuild the nation in 2019. She had deserved the salute and it was he who had finally given it to her. The smile stayed on his face as the watch officer approached.

Chapter 4

Lieut. Gen Darwin sat in one of the chairs alongside the wall in the president's cabinet room listening to the briefer. The president had not attended the meeting which did not surprise her. Unless a major decision of some type had to be addressed or a crisis was occurring, he had his senior staff run the daily situation briefings. Those in the White House and new members quickly learned that the new president did not like to attend meetings. He had his staff do it by proxy and condense the information down to a one-page summary. The other thing they all learned was that the president was almost incapable of deciding anything on his own. He would bring in whomever was involved with the problem, let them as a group come up with the final solution and only after all of them had agreed on what action to take did, he finally take a stance.

Wendy knew that if major crises should occur that required immediate action this president was not capable of doing it. Thank God she thought, at least he has extremely competent people around him and in all the cabinet posts. When the meeting was over, she rose from her chair and started for the door.

Ed Manson, the president's chief of staff spoke her name. "General Darwin, the president would like to see you in his office."

As she moved into the oval office, the president rose from his desk and advanced toward her with that charming smile on his face. He was a handsome man in his late fifties and easily looked like a movie star. That was one of the major reasons he had been elected president of the United States, at least that was what Wendy thought. The two had not hit it off since their first meeting and Wendy had thought that he would have her reassigned to another position outside the White House but that had not happened and she was not sure why. He preferred yes-men around him and she was far from that. So, she figured maybe this was the swan song for her departure.

Instead, the president surprised her. "Wendy I will be the first to admit that we have not exactly seen eye-to-eye on some of the issues since I came into this office but I want you to know I respect your judgment and the position you hold. Most importantly, you are one of the few people in this nation who has the background and experience of what happened in this country for the past twenty years."

Wendy was not sure exactly where all this was going until he asked. "What did you make of that telephone call you received this morning?"

Now Wendy knew what was coming and she was not surprised. "Mr. President. I believe this country may very well be in grave danger of a terrorist attack on our country in the days to come. The phone call only reinforces it. My contact is reliable and has been for many years and he would not have taken the risk of calling me if he did not think it was urgent."

The president watched her for moment and she could see the indecision in his eyes. She waited. And then he surprised her again. "All right, General Darwin, I want you to take full control of this situation and you will only report to me. We cannot afford to have another major terrorist attack on this country and it is going to be your job to make sure it does not happen."

He then handed her the transcript of the phone call she had taken earlier in the day and turned back to his desk. The meeting was over, no discussion, no feedback, no real comments from him.

Back at her desk, Wendy realized he had wiped the whole issue from his hands and left it up to her to resolve. It should not have surprised her and it didn't. She glanced down at the transcript and then reread it.

"Good morning, Wendy, I hope you are well."

"That's good of you to say, Ehson. Allah has been good to me since we last saw each other."

"That is good," Ehson replied. "I only have a few moments and must leave but I wanted to let you know that several of your family members will take up your invitation to visit within a few days. I will provide more details later. I must go for now."

"Thank you for your thoughtfulness, Ehson. I will look forward to hearing from you soon."

"Go with God," he replied and the phone connection went dead.

The note she had dictated to the watch officer followed:

Mr. President, the phone call was from an old and trusted friend. The message was in fact a warning that a terrorist cell may well strike this country again in the next few days. Lieutenant General Darwin

COLD WIND

What she had not told the president or anyone else was the man she had talked with was from the far past. She had not heard from him in over ten years and it had brought back memories of that cold desert night when her F 31 jet fighter had crashed in the desert. The cold wind had hit her hard as she climbed out of the plane and then she saw the man standing there watching her. She had almost shot him. For the next ten days the two of them had played a game of hide and seek with her pursuers and if it had not been for Ehson she knew she would have died before help arrived.

She also knew Ehson's real name and had watched his rise to power over the years. His name is well known throughout the Arab world. Aariz Monoman is the Deputy Prime Minister of the newly created Republic of Carush, a small but very powerful new country in the Middle East. The prime objective of this new regime was to destroy Israel by any means possible and the United States was second on their list. Yet that information did not detour Wendy from believing in the message she had received from this man.

A bond formed between the two of them during those ten days in the desert; one that she knew would never break. The threat was real and it was now up to her to stop whatever these people had planned.

When Chief of Staff Manson had asked how the man was able to contact her, she had replied, "I have a special telephone number tied into all the computers in the White House, Department of Defense and all the intelligence agencies. If that number comes up, it is automatically forwarded to me no matter where I am."

"Oh," was all he said.

As soon as Wendy left the oval office, the chief of staff walked in and detected that President Baker was upset. That was a bad sign. He stood just inside the doorway and watched the president as he walked back and forth behind the desk.

Finally, he stopped pacing and asked, "How valid do you think that threat is Ed?"

"As you know, Mr. President, there have been very few threats against this country in the past twenty years and all of them were minor, involving only one or two groups. None of them succeeded. They caught all of them and they are now no longer with us. Justice has been swift for anyone who has attempted to do harm to our country. This threat could be some of the same. Just a threat."

The president replied in an agitated tone, "If the information had come from anyone other than General Darwin I might agree with you, Ed, but she is a military hero. Christ! She is a national hero and if I fail to take her seriously and then an attack on this country should occur, I would be the one who will be blamed."

Ed Manson thought to himself, well he's being true to form. He's not worried about anyone but himself.

"I have given General Darwin full authority to pursue this threat but I want you to assign someone to monitor what she is doing and that individual will only report to you."

What he really means is he wants a spy. But *why* Ed didn't understand.

****

Special Agent Nick Protelly slowly hung up the phone and walked over to the large electronic screen that had a map of the United States displayed. He looked at the blue line that began in Lansing Michigan and traveled down I-69 to I-80/90 then west toward South Bend, Indiana and through Gary, Indiana where it separates and goes into I-80 and continued to Davenport and Iowa City. There it had turned north on I-380 toward Cedar Rapids. Once out of that city the blue line paralleled a secondary road Highway 30 and moved west again where it connected with the small city of Ames. From there the blue line ran south and it stopped in the city of Des Moines, Iowa.

With the loss of the satellite, Nick's agents could only follow the transmitter installed on the rental vehicle before the man had picked it up and in the dark it was impossible to follow too close. Within minutes of finding out that the car was no longer in motion, the agents found the car abandoned and their target had vanished. All he could do was flood the city with agents and hope they could pick up his trail again or ascertain if Des Moines was the courier's final destination. He had a feeling about this case and knew they had better find this man.

It was June 4th and General Darwin sat in the conference room in the bunker waiting for her visitors to arrive. She had two folders lying side by side on the table and her fingers lightly touched one of them. She looked at the wall clock. It was one of the digital types that move from left to right on a continuous basis. It read 3:58 p.m. June 4, 2040. A few minutes later her two visitors arrived. Both men in full dress uniform stood in front of her at the edge of the table, saluted and in unison declared, "Reporting as ordered, Ma'am."

She could see the ever-so-slight smile on the man to the left and a serious look on the man to the right. Both men were handsome in different ways. Lieutenant Norm Shepherd, Jr. had the looks of his father, the light brown skin highlighted the dark brown eyes. Built like his father, he stood six-feet two-inches tall and approximately one hundred eighty pounds, all muscle. The other man was of Arabic descent; black flashing eyes and just a faint hint of a beard. His skin tone was much like Norm's but that was where the comparison stopped. He was five-feet eight-inches tall and weighed around one hundred sixty pounds, and like Norm he appeared to be all muscle. She of course knew both these men, one all his life and the other for about ten years. Wendy had sponsored him and his mother when they came to this country after his father had died while supporting American special forces in a classified mission in the Middle East. It was a mission she had directly been involved in. She returned their salute and motioned for them to sit.

Both Arydin and Norm had graduated from the Naval Academy ranking number one and two respectfully in their class. Lieutenant Arydin Hassan beat Norm out by one percentage point. Since their first days at the Academy, they had become close friends and it had been Wendy who had introduced them to each other. In fact, it had been Wendy who had paved the way for Arydin to attend the Academy. There had been stiff opposition against his admission. The distrust of any Moslem was still very strong within the country but she had prevailed and he was accepted. Norm had an automatic pass into the academy because his father had received a Medal of Honor.

After graduation their assignment was to a highly classified intelligence unit within the Pentagon and again it had been General Darwin who had directed that moved. If either man knew of her actions, they never mentioned it to her.

"How is your mother, Ross? I have not seen her for a while."

"She's fine, ma'am," Ross replied.

She looked at Arydin, "And yours? Is she still sending you those delicious cookies?"

"Yes, ma'am," he replied. "She's well and I left some of those cookies with the watch officer for you."

"I'm not sure how many will be left before I can rescue them," Wendy replied with a smile. Then she tapped both folders in front of her and said, "Right now, both of you are being reassigned to a classified program code-named 'Ehsan.'" Arydin's eyes widened for just a second but Norm maintained a neutral expression.

Norm asked, "How many others are involved in this program?"

"Only the two of you."

"Whom will we be reporting to?" Arydin asked.

"Me." She replied and saw the surprise flicker across both their faces. "It is my belief that there is a terrorist cell from the Middle East already inside the country or soon will be. And whatever their mission is we cannot allow it to be achieved."

Wendy looked at Arydin. "If you have any reservations about this assignment now is the time to tell me." She saw the hurt look in his eyes and almost wished she hadn't asked the question.

"General Darwin, I may be a Moslem, but I am an American and will defend this country with my life if it should come to that and no matter whom the terrorists are."

She had her answer and it was no less than she expected. "Very well, I want the two of you to find out who these people are, where they're located and what they plan to do. And then I want you to destroy them."

Both men had the same thought, God, she doesn't want much. But they knew she expected just that.

Chapter 5

Rush-hour traffic caught the two men driving back to the Pentagon. Norm glanced over at Arydin who was attempting to move into the left lane but was having no success. Muttering under his breath, Arydin finally rolled down the side window and stuck his arm out gesturing to the driver beside him that he wanted to turn into that lane. The driver reluctantly slowed down and Arydin quickly moved in front of him still muttering in Arabic. Norm had learned the language years ago at the insistence of General Darwin and could speak and write the language as well as Arydin.

Norm turned to his friend, "They may be crazy DC drivers but they are no worse than those camel drivers I have seen in Cairo." And both men burst out laughing. Norm could sense that Arydin was still smarting over General Darwin's direct questions but he also knew she never asked a question just for the sake of asking. She had a reason even if she already knew the answer.

As if reading his mind Arydin asked, "You have any idea why she put me on the spot like that? Hell, she has been my benefactor for the past ten years and I think she knows me as well as my own mother. It just does not make sense to me why she did that." Norm decided to keep his mouth shut and let Arydin figure it out for himself.

As they inched forward in the traffic, his thoughts drifted to the famous female general who was almost like an icon to the public and even more so to the men and women who served in the armed forces. His memories were on a more personal basis simply because she had been a part of his life for as long as he could remember. When he was ten years-old he had come home from school one day and asked his mother why she and General Darwin were such good friends and in almost the same breath he stated she is white and we are black. He had seen the startled look on his mother's face before her hands had flown to her face and she had burst into tears. He knew he had hurt her deeply but he didn't know why.

When she finally stopped crying, she had looked at him in a way he had never seen before. Without a word she had taken his hand and led him to her bedroom. As he sat on the bed, she went to the closet and came back holding a dozen or so photo albums. Over the next two hours, she told him stories of his father and Wendy Darwin, stories that only a handful of people had ever heard.

He learned things on a more personal basis about his famous father and how Wendy had taken his mother under her wing when she arrived at the White House. It was she who had helped during his birth and who sheltered his mother in those trying days. A fiercely strong bond had formed between the two women; one that was apparent to all that knew them.

When his mother finished, she looked straight into her son's eyes and said, "Wendy does not look at me and see black and I do not look at her and see white. There is no race difference between us, only two women who love each other." Norm learned a lesson that day and he never forgot it.

From that day forward, he followed Wendy's career every chance he got. He would pester his mother and Wendy every time he had the chance and his admiration grew through the years.

****

After the attack which devastated the country and killed over two hundred million of its citizens, Wendy had worked closely with General McKay in rebuilding the country's military armed forces. When President Singleton completed her term, the government was still in the throes of rebuilding its Air Force and Wendy now a major in the Marine Corps entered flight school. She started flying the country's newest jet fighters and quickly rose to the rank of colonel.

After another stint in the White House, she returned to the now combined United States Air Force as commander of one of the newest jet squadrons. Within months of taking command, the squadron was deployed to the Middle East to support Israel. That country had suddenly been attacked by several Middle East countries.

The air battles were vicious and the coalition forces were outnumbered ten to one, but with the arrival of Colonel Darwin's squadron the tide slowly turned. Within two weeks Darwin was an ace and as the conflict ended her kill rate had increased to seventeen. The American public was fascinated by her fighting skill. The news of her being shot down in a dogfight was shocking.

Wendy had been outnumbered six to one but had downed another four-enemy aircraft before her fighter jet went down making her an ace four times over.

From the reports that had filtered in the dog fight had occurred deep in enemy territory and when hit she had sent a mayday and then only silence. The country was in mourning some ten days later when it learned that she had survived. A Navy Seal team had rescued her somewhere in the desert. Upon returning to the United States, she was promoted to brigadier general and awarded the Medal of Honor.

The news media was in a feeding-frenzy and for weeks tried to find out how she had survived in the desert alone. All she would say was that a missile had struck close by her aircraft and her engine had flamed out but she had been able to land in the desert. What she would not say, and the military kept the secret, was the circumstances of her escape and rescue. All she would say was the information needed to be classified to ensure other pilots forced down in enemy territory would not be compromised.

The Air Force chief of staff and the Air Force accident investigation board were also left out as to what had happened simply because she refused to tell them. That did not make the brass very happy and when they started to put the pressure on her, Wendy had quietly called in some very high chips. The investigation inquiry was closed. Wendy had known if she had exposed Ehson as the man who had saved her life, he would have probably lost his. That was something she was not willing to take a chance on. Only she and Ehson knew what happened during the ten days she was in the desert.

Chapter 6

Agent Protelly stood in front of the map on the screen as he briefed the two men concerning the courier his team had been tracking. When the blue line, depicting the travel routes, came to a stop he pointed to the city and said, "We lost him yesterday, June 5, in Des Moines Iowa."

While looking at the map Ross asked, "What are the chances of finding him?"

"It's hard to tell," the agent replied, "but we do have some pluses. This morning we have over one hundred agents in the city looking for him and his contact or contacts. If he is still in the city, we have a good chance of finding him."

Arydin asked," What makes you think that?"

Agent Protelly moved to his desk and picked up a folder. He studied it for a moment then looked at both men. With a hard-edge to his voice he explained, "Prior to the last attack on our country, Des Moines, Iowa had a population of some two hundred thousand people and the surrounding countryside, within this county, had approximately five hundred thousand. During the attack the city lost over 75 percent of its population, some one hundred-fifty thousand souls. The county faired out a little better. It only lost around 50 percent and the death toll in that area was around two-hundred-fifty thousand citizens. With that said the city of Des Moines now has a population of approximately sixty thousand and the county two hundred-seventy thousand. With a city that size and the small population, we have a good chance of spotting the courier if he should attempt to move around. The problem is if he has already left the city, we may never find him."

He turned back to the map and drew a circle around the city. "We have expanded the search area some four hundred miles outside the city and as I speak, I have some five hundred agents moving into the cities and towns in that area. This includes Sioux City, Iowa which is now the state capital."

"Based on what you have said and the resources you've allocated to this search, what makes this man so important?" Arydin asked.

Agent Protelly hesitated for a second as if not sure how to answer and then stated, "He is a Shia national who has been suspected of having ties

21

with Al Qaeda. We couldn't prove it so he was never detained. He showed up in Lansing Michigan about ten years ago as a refugee from somewhere in Afghanistan. We think he was around ten years of age at that time. Documentation on his background is almost nonexistent. We have never been able to determine if he had any relatives in the area and a local member of the Muslim community assumed the responsibility for raising him."

He continued, "The guardian probably had another motive for doing so because he was soon put to work in the man's pizza parlor. There is one puzzling fact though. When he arrived in Lansing, he told everyone that his name was Harris and it's the name he still goes by to this day."

"Why is that so strange?" Norm asked.

Arydin spoke up, "Norm, in the Muslim world a male boy is given a name that he keeps until he reaches manhood, normally around twelve to fourteen years of age and then he is given another name which he keeps for the rest of his life."

"OK," Norm stated, "but what makes this guy so special?"

"It appears that this individual was never given another name," Protelly answered. "That's highly unusual in the Muslim world. To our knowledge and in the community, he has always just been called Harris. That raised a red flag within the Bureau and over the years we have been keeping him under surveillance more than most. Our surveillance has increased more in the past three years. As a boy he worked in the pizza parlor of his benefactor and then about three years ago he started delivering pizza throughout the city. It was shortly after that, the Bureau started to notice a pattern in the delivery process. Although he delivered pizza all over the city, in the past two years almost all of those delivers, some 75 percent, has been to mosques within the city. His deliveries happened several times a day. Our agents also noticed that many times he stayed in the mosques much longer than required to deliver the pizza. It was then that the Bureau believed he was delivering not only pizza but messages between the various mosques. The question is why?"

"We assume he is a courier and when suddenly he began delivering outside the city, which he had never done before, we staged a full-scale surveillance on him. He has no relation that we know of outside the city and it automatically raised red flags with our people."

"I do not understand your logic," Arydin stated. "Just because some Arab travels between mosque in Michigan does not tell me the man is a terrorist."

"You may be right, Lieutenant Arydin, but twenty years ago Islamic Arabs killed some two hundred million Americans and, if I have any control over what this man is up to, I will do whatever is possible to make sure he fails. If it had not been on the direct orders of General Darwin, I would assure you that I would not have provided you this information today."

Arydin could see and hear Agent Protelly's anger as he answered the question. "Furthermore, I do not understand nor do I like the idea of either of you having access to my agents in the field and more important you having control over them. You should also know that I voiced my objection but the director overruled me. His orders were very explicit, give you all the support I can or go find another job. Therefore, what do you want from me?"

Chapter 7

Darkness was closing in as the courier drove through the northside of the city and although fully briefed on where the transfer would take place, he still had ten minutes before his contact would arrive. It gave him a few more minutes to make sure no one was following. Finally, he turned down a tree lined street with houses on both sides but most did not have lights burning. Many houses were unoccupied which included the last four on the right-side of the street. As he pulled over to the curb, he saw the lights of a truck slowly pull up beside his vehicle. The courier slid out his vehicle and opened the door of the pickup before it'd come to a complete stop. He quickly got in and shut the door and turned to the driver. He was surprised that it was a woman but held the slight resentment within him. It must be Allah's will or she would not be here. The only words spoken between them were when she asked is Allah near. And he had answered no but soon. With that both knew who the other was. The vehicle started moving and she made a right turn at the next corner. Within minutes they were out of the area where he had left the car.

It was already too late for the FBI agents who had moved in behind the car only to find it empty. As the alert went out, the pickup was already on I-35 heading north toward Mason City, Iowa, about one hundred-twenty miles away.

There was little traffic on the interstate at this time of the evening but there were enough vehicles on the road that they blended in with the flow of traffic. The courier knew that with night coming on the traffic would ease and make them more conspicuous and that thought made him uneasy. But he kept the thought to himself. He pulled out a pack of cigarettes from his shirt pocket and lit one and slowly blew the smoke from his mouth. The woman opened her side window an inch or so but kept her eyes on the road ahead.

He could tell the woman did not like him smoking and he thought again women should not be part of this operation but there was nothing he could do about it now.

Chapter 8

Arydin and Norm had spent most of the morning of June 6 in the FBI field office in Des Moines watching the dragnet unfold on the large state map. If nothing else the FBI was incredibly fast and efficient in moving its people in place but up until now no leads had surfaced on the suspects' whereabouts.

As Arydin and Norm returned from lunch, the agent in charge of the hunt said, "I think we may have something. The state police just notified us of a multiple murder in the town of Seaton, Iowa which is about fifteen miles from the Canadian border. That is about one hundred ten miles from Des Moines. I have a helicopter waiting. Come on, I will brief you as we go."

At first neither man could see any connection between the murders and the manhunt for their suspect, that is until the agent stated it appears two of the victims, a man and a woman, were of Middle Eastern descent. That caught their attention real fast.

It seemed that a George Baker had made an unexpected stop at his elderly parent's home just outside of Seaton early this morning and when he could not find them, he became concerned and called the local sheriff's office. Since neither parent was able to drive, someone had to pick them up, maybe a friend or neighbor. At least that was what he thought until he found a strange pickup parked behind the shed.

From the State police report it was not too long after the sheriff arrived that one of the deputies discovered a pool of blood in the kitchen pantry. After a thorough search of the house, they went to inspect the shed and pickup. As soon as they approached the vehicle, the sheriff saw the fresh dirt under it and had the vehicle towed a few yards away. It was apparent that something was buried there and not long ago. The top soil was still moist. It was here that they found the bodies of an unidentified man and woman in addition to Mr. and Mrs. Baker. At this point the sheriff contacted the state police.

The authorities at the shed watched as the helicopter circled the house and then land in a field a few hundred yards from the house. After inspecting the gravesite, Arydin had pulled a map up on his cellphone showing it to Norm. He said, "There is a fairly large community of Muslims just north of here in Alberta

Canada and if I had to guess that is where these two came from," and he pointed to the two unidentified bodies lying on the ground.

****

When Norm and Arydin returned to the field office in Des Moines, they found that Arydin's hunch had been correct. The fingerprints of the dead man and woman had been uploaded and transmitted to FBI headquarters in Washington and the results were now before them. The two folders of information included pictures of the man and woman and a short summary on each.

****

The FBI agent stated, "We're moving our people into that area now to see if we can flush anyone out. The Canadian government has approved our incursion into their country and are working closely with us."

Arydin replied, "I hope you are right but I doubt anyone is there." Then he turned and walked to the large map on the screen.

Norm came up beside him and asked, "Why don't you think he is there, Arydin?"

Arydin didn't say anything for several moments and then pointed to a spot on the map. "If the Muslim community was his destination then why go to all the effort of killing the old couple and set up a meeting some fifteen or twenty miles away? That does not make sense. Hell, they could have just drove him up there. I think they were not taking any chances of the man being spotted in the area so they picked an out-of-the-way place to meet and provide whatever information they had. The only thing I don't understand is why he killed them. Second, if he did not go to a mosque then which way did he go?"

Again, he pointed at the map and as if musing to himself said, "He could have gotten what he came for and turned back east heading back to Lansing, Michigan. But I don't think so. Or he could have doubled back heading south but I think with the number of FBI agents now covering this area he would have been spotted."

"So that leaves him heading west," Norm replied.

"Yeah, but to where?" Arydin questioned.

"Well, we know one thing, he's getting help from people associated with mosques and there are very few mosques left in this part of the country," Norm stated and picked up the phone.

Ten minutes later Norm had the location of every mosque in the country broken down by state in his lap top, most were located in major cities or grouped close together. As the two men looked at North and South Dakota they started placing flags as identifiers on the map. It did not take long. There were only three mosques located in North Dakota and five in South Dakota.

Norm asked, "What doesn't look right to you Arydin?"

Arydin pointed to the state of South Dakota and saw there were two mosques located at the state capital in Pierre and two in Sioux Falls. Both large cities for that state but then he moved his finger down to the lower part of the state to the lone flag located next to the town of Winner, South Dakota.

"That mosque is way out in no-man's-land and there is no rationale that I can think of for it being there. It's out of character for Muslim communities to do that."

Norm stated, "I saw that too but wanted to see if you felt the same way. Let's see what information is available about it." And again, he reached for the phone.

A few minutes later they had their information including a question from FBI Agent Nick Protelly. He had simply asked what is so interesting about Winner, South Dakota?

Arydin laughed, "I think he's beginning to like us."

"Fat chance," Norman replied.

"Well, there's not much there. The town had a population of some four thousand prior to the attack on the country and now the population is less than five hundred souls. It's farming country and no industry is available except for one granary. It seems that a small group of Arabic men, nine in all, left the mosque in Sioux Falls seven months ago and relocated to Winner. They bought some acreage just outside of town and paid cash for it – two hundred forty-six thousand dollars. They tend to stay to themselves and that's about all that's known about them."

FBI Agent Protelly said, "There's been one follow-up by one of the agents to the area and that was three months ago."

"So where does that leave us?" Arydin asked.

"Not sure. I have a feeling we need to visit Winner, South Dakota but first I want to visit the mosque in Sioux Falls or I should say you need to."

"Why me?" Arydin asked.

With a playful grin, Norm answered, "The last I knew you were a Moslem and know your way around a mosque. If I were to go, they would probably stop me before I got in the front door. We need to find out who those nine men are. I know it's a longshot but it's all I can think of unless you have a better idea. I think time is running out."

****

It was noon when they arrived in Sioux Falls and were escorted to the FBI's command center. Arydin checked out the street address of the mosque, found it on the city map and left.

Norm sent a reply to FBI Agent Protelly stating although there was no hard evidence to go on regarding the mosque in Winner, South Dakota he and Arydin planned on going there before nightfall and he did not want the FBI to send any agents to the town prior to their arrival.

What he did ask for was four FBI SWAT teams to be deployed as soon as possible to the towns of Colome, Witten, Lucas and Hamill. Three of which were approximately fifteen miles from Winner, the other Lucas being thirty miles away. This way the town would be boxed-in and if trouble should arise it would take only a few minutes for the SWAT teams to arrive or block escape routes.

Norm did not want to alert those individuals at the mosque especially if the courier planned on going there. He looked at his watch and knew their suspect would have ample time to reach Winner by night fall if he did not stop. Norm finished his situation report and transmitter it to Lieutenant General Wendy Darwin.

Some three hours later he was going over the FBI situation report when Arydin walked in.

Wendy Darwin felt the tension build in her body as she read Norm's situation report and hoped the two men could complete their mission and return safely. She also knew the alternative and how would she tell their mothers.

****

When the woman reached their destination at Seaton, Iowa it was dark. No vehicle traffic was on the roads as they drove through town and pulled into the driveway of a small cottage. There were no other homes located nearby.

She pulled around to the back and only one light suddenly came on from the corner of the house. Harris saw the man standing in the doorway.

His driver stated, "You must be hungry. I will prepare a meal and Akil will brief you on the information we have received in support of your journey."

After they finished the meal and the information was passed to him, he turned to the couple and asked, "Where are the people who lived here?"

The man answered, "We were told to leave no one alive that might be able to provide information regarding you. I killed them this afternoon when I arrived. We have had this house under surveillance for several days and knew the old couple lived here alone. If we are lucky no one will find out they're dead for several days and by then we will all be gone."

"Where did you put the bodies?" Harris asked.

The man pointed to the pantry and said, "They're in there."

Harris shook his head and stated, "It would be too easy to find them. Can we bury them outback of the house?"

"Of course, if that is what you wish."

An hour later, the three of them stood looking down into the hole with the old couple now lying in it.

Harris then turned to Akil and asked, "Is that blue van the one you used to come here?"

Akil replied, "Yes." Then Harris shot him and his woman companion.

After placing them in the hole with the old couple, he covered the bodies with dirt and moved the pickup over the grave to hide the freshly-dug earth.

Twenty minutes later, he finished cleaning up and laid down on the sofa. As he fell asleep, his last thoughts were Akil had been right, no one was exempt from dying to protect his mission.

Chapter 9

The courier made good time after leaving Seaton, Iowa but was careful not to draw attention to himself or the blue van. By 10 a.m. he arrived in the small Iowa town of Sibley. Following the directions given to him he pulled into the driveway of a small cottage just outside of town. He took a set of keys from his pocket and stepped out of the van and waited a moment before walking to the garage.

Inside was a new black Buick LaCrosse and with the keys inside his pocket, he pressed the starter and drove it outside. Parking the car, he returned to the van and drove it inside the garage, closed the door and drove off in the car. The switch took less than five minutes and he saw no one as he left the area.

At Benson, Iowa, he turned onto Route 12 and crossed over into South Dakota where he connected with I-29 south toward Sioux Falls, South Dakota. He was hungry but knew he dared not stop. Then he remembered the food and water placed in the trunk for his use. He pulled the car over, opened the trunk and saw the bottled water and paper sack. A few minutes later he was on his way.

****

Norm listened until Arydin finished talking then stated, "That doesn't sound good. You would have thought that the leader of the mosque would have been more helpful."

"I agree, Norm, but I had the feeling he was scared to death."

"So, what we have is nine men, individually or in small groups, showing up at this mosque over a three-month period. All were vague as to why they came here, tended to stay by themselves and then suddenly seven months ago decided to set up their own mosque in Winner, South Dakota. Why?" Norm stated.

"I don't know but let's go find out," Arydin replied.

Just before they left, Norm sent a message to FBI Agent Protelly requesting all the information the agency had on those nine men.

****

ED Manson, the president's chief of staff, could see President Baker was in one of his bad moods and decided it was better to just keep his mouth shut.

Finally, the president asked, "What do you make of this?" He slammed the folder down on the desk.

"Sir, it looks like we have one man, a Moslem, traveling across the country and the FBI in pursuit but we don't know what he's up to or why."

"Well, I know one thing," the president replied, "he's starting to leave a trail of dead bodies in his wake," and he pointed at the folder on his desk. "If the news media gets ahold of this there will be hell to pay. So far, we've been able to keep it under wraps but for how long? And who are these two military men appearing to run the show?"

"From what I understand, Sir, General Darwin made the assignment and when I questioned her about it, she stated that the president gave her full authority to pursue this threat and that's what she is doing. She also said she had given those two men explicit orders; find out who these people are, where they're located, what they plan to do and if they are a threat, to destroy them."

"My God, the president said as he sat down. She can't do that."

"Well. Sir, unless you take her out of this situation which I strongly recommend you don't, she has your authority to pursue it. There is also another point to consider, Sir. If this turns out to be a terrorist attack and they succeed then you have a scapegoat to take the heat."

"What do you mean?" the president asked.

"Sir, as soon as you found out that there may be a terrorist cell in our country you ordered General Darwin, with your full authority, to apprehend them. If she fails the blame will be on her, not you."

Ed saw the sly smile form on the corners of the president's mouth as he let that sink in. He addressed Ed as he stood up, "Just keep me informed." And the meeting was over.

Ed could feel the knot in his stomach as he walked down the hall and thought, the bastard didn't even ask if the threat was real or what we should do to protect the population if it should occur. At least I have given General Darwin more time. If anyone can resolve this threat in our favor it's her. I have no doubt the president would have removed her if I had not planted that seed, and he smiled as he continued walking down the hall.

COLD WIND

Prior to leaving the FBI operations center in Sioux Falls both Norm and Arydin had not been carrying firearms. Now they armed themselves, along with bulletproof vests and FBI radios. Each now carried a 45 mm handgun and Norm had a semi-automatic rifle. Arydin had a sniper's rifle. Both men were trained at the Academy and considered formidable with the weaponry but neither had ever shot at another human being let alone killed anyone.

Now as they were nearing Winner, Norm pulled the car over and off the road. The sun was starting to set in the west and he knew it would be dark within an hour.

Arydin had left the car and was standing by a ditch looking at the landscape. Turning to Norm he stated with a wave of his hand, "Well, we can't just drive up to the mosque. They could see us coming five miles away. The land around here is flat as a pancake and whatever they're growing it's only two or three feet high."

"It's called sorghum, Arydin, and you're right we are not going to be able to just drive up and ask to be invited in."

"So, what have you got in mind, Norm?"

"Unless you have a better idea why don't we drive into Winner, find the local law enforcement officer and convince him or her to drive us by that farmhouse just after dark? We'll make sure the vehicle is a pickup or farm truck so when it slows down, we can jump out the back. I guess from there we play it by ear."

Arydin laughed, "Some plan but you're right. I can't think of anything better. What are we going to do when we get there, just say hands up and arrest them?"

"That's just what I am hoping for, Arydin, because if we can get close enough before we're spotted, we might just have a chance of surprising them before they have time to react."

"What about our FBI backup guys?"

"Only if we need them. Hell, the two of us ought to be able to handle nine guys."

Arydin just smiled and got back into the car.

****

Agent Protelly stood looking at a large map of South Dakota along with several other men and he was a very unhappy man and really pissed off. The satellite photos posted on the wall showed the teams he had established for Norm and one showing Norm and Arydin's exact location.

The satellite photo that concerned him the most was one that depicted the farmhouse and a late model black Buick LaCrosse. He looked at the date on the bottom of the photo which showed the vehicle had arrived at 4:27 p.m., June 6, 2040.

But what was really getting him upset was the results he was getting from Norm's request for additional information on the nine men. He had flooded the areas from which the men had lived prior to moving to Sioux Falls with many agents and a pattern was beginning to emerge that they were not who they portrayed to be. Three of the men had used names of individuals who were dead and the other six had used names of unsuspecting individuals who were alive.

He felt the cold chill run through his body and he reached for the phone.

****

Norm slowly returned his cell phone to his belt clip and turned to Arydin. "Well, my friend, it looks like we're going to have company with us tonight. That was Agent Protelly and he's moving his teams to our location now. They should all be here within thirty minutes."

"Why the change of plans?" Arydin replied.

"Well, it seems none of the nine Moslems are who they claim to be and they had a visitor arrive this afternoon. Agent Protelly believes it may be the courier. He is also sending additional agents as fast as he can get them here."

"So, do we call off the trip to the farmhouse for now?"

"No," Norm replied. "Agent Protelly thinks we should not take the chance that the courier might slip away after dark and I agree with him. The only thing that changes is we'll have more firepower when we go in."

"Norm, suddenly I have a bad feeling."

"So, do I, Arydin, so do I," he repeated.

Chapter 10

The nine men inside the house sat on prayer blankets listening to the courier when suddenly a small red light started blinking over the door. Without a word one of them went to a closet and started handing out weapons. As the courier watched, one of the men explained, "We have detection devices surrounding the house and something has tripped one of them. It could be nothing as it happens every so often because of a deer, dog or some other animal, but we cannot take any chances. You need to go." The courier stood and followed the man into the next room.

Norm and Arydin were laying side-by-side in the sorghum field only a few hundred feet from the farmhouse when they heard a warning on their FBI radios, "They have sensors all over the place and now we must assume they know we're here. Go, go, go."

As they rose to charge the farmhouse, gunfire erupted from the windows and doors. Arydin saw two agents fall and he dove back to the rifle and looking through the night scope saw the silhouette of a man firing a weapon from one of the upper windows. He would quickly fire a burst and move to his right out of sight only to return a few seconds later and fire again.

Fine Arydin thought, so let's do it the hard way and he put the crosshairs of the rifle just to the right of the window a foot above the window seal and waited. The gunman fired again and as he moved out of sight Arydin fired two shots into the side of the house. Seconds later the man came crashing through the window still firing the gun as he fell to the ground. That's what I call a fanatic, Arydin thought as he started crawling forward looking for Norm.

Several agents had gained access to the farmhouse and Arydin could hear the continuous gunfire as he worked his way beside the house. As a figure burst out a side door, Arydin dropped to the ground as the bullets whizzed past his head. He knew he was a dead man because the man would fire again before he could raise the rifle. Then he heard a 45-caliber gun go off five times in quick succession and saw the gunman flung back into the building.

Out of nowhere, Norm was at his side asking if he was all right.

"Yes, but I would have been full of holes if you had not showed up."

"Well partner that's what friends are for. Now let's get inside and find out what's going on. It seems the firefight is over."

As they cautiously moved through the first floor of the farmhouse, they could see the carnage of what had taken place. Arydin walked over to one FBI agent laying on the floor in a large pool of blood. He checked for a pulse and there was none. Lying under him was another man in a robe. Arydin started to bend down to check for a pulse and jerked back as the man's eyes opened.

Norm kicked the machine gun away from the man's outstretched hand and Arydin again bent down and looked into the man's eyes and then asked, "Why?"

A glint of pure hatred flashed in the man's eyes as he replied, "You will all die. Allah is great," he shouted, then shuddered and died.

The sound of his voice brought two FBI agents rushing through the door with guns drawn.

"Take it easy guys. Remember we're on your side," Norm yelled.

As they lowered their weapons one of them said, "We just did a sweep of this room and thought everyone in here was dead. When we heard someone speaking in Arabic, we thought we had missed one of them down here because we cannot account for one of them yet." Then with a tinge of bitterness in his voice he asked, "You talk their language, what did he say?"

Norm replied, "You will all die. Allah is great."

The agent turned sharply toward Norm. He was surprised since he had directed the question to Arydin but Norm had translated.

Then all of them heard the orders coming through the FBI radios they carried. "Everyone, pick up our dead and wounded and get out of the house. It's rigged with explosives and could go at any time. Get the hell out of there now!"

Arydin bent down and gently picked up the dead FBI agent and moved to the door followed by the other two agents and Norm.

Dashing through the sorghum field, Arydin refused to allow either Norm or the other two agents to help carry the dead agent. It was not until a gigantic explosion that caused them all to fall to the ground did Arydin start weeping while still holding the dead FBI agent in his arms.

****

Fifteen hours later a debriefing was held at the community church in Winner. Sitting at the head table were Norm, Arydin and FBI Agent Protelly. All the other agents sat in the pews. With a seating capacity of one hundred fifty, it was still too small for the three hundred plus agents now present in Winner, South Dakota and the number was still growing.

The meeting had been going on for some time and finally Agent Protelly stood up and said, "This is not working. We need to break our teams down to small groups. Let them work the issues and then funnel their findings back to the core group. That way we can see the whole picture. All team chiefs gather your personnel and find a place in town where you can work. The town fathers say you can have whatever you want. It will have to do until we received the large tents the military is bringing. They should be here by nightfall with food, sleeping and medical facilities."

Then Protelly stood and turned to Norm and Arydin. "We need to talk," and he moved to the door.

Ten minutes later the three of them sat in a booth in the only diner in town staring at each other. With coffee cups in front of them, none of them had spoken.

Finally, Protelly signed then said, "All right, I owe both of you an apology. I was wrong. When I was told by my supervisor to provide whatever support you required, it went against the grain of my agency and more importantly myself. I forgot to look at the whole picture. I did not realize the grave danger we are in but both of you did. When we lost track of the courier, I thought it wouldn't take long to find him and when we did the situation would be resolved in short order. I was wrong. We didn't find him, but you two did. Arydin, I owe you a personal apology. I was resentful of the fact that a Moslem would oversee tracking another Moslem and I did not trust you. I also heard what you did for that agent of mine and I will never forget it. Agent Brimes was a friend of mine and at least his wife and children will have his body to bury. I don't believe we would have found enough of him to bury if you had not recovered his body. I cannot thank you enough for that."

Arydin looked thoughtfully at the man for a moment and then replied, "Agent Protelly, I love this country just like you do. I would die defending it, just like your agent did and no apologies are necessary."

Protelly acknowledged the statement and then looked at Norm. "Lieutenant Shepherd, I think we may have a problem. So far, we have lost three agents and two wounded which is bad enough but what we have been able to determine is that our people brought out the bodies of nine Moslem men before that farmhouse was destroyed. That leaves one man still missing if the courier arrived yesterday afternoon and I believe he did."

"Agent Protelly, call me Norm."

"Fair enough," Protelly replied then stated, "the Buick we found in the barn was severely damaged by the blast but we were able to determine it had been stolen several days ago from a couple who lives in Alberta, Canada not far from the mosque that two of our dead individuals were from. That's too much of a coincidence. The man was in that farmhouse last night and so far, we can't find him or for that matter any part of him. We had that area so sealed up it would have been impossible for anyone to have slipped through the net. So where in the hell is he?"

"I agree with your assessment, Protelly, but somehow the man is gone," Norm replied, "and somehow, we need to find him because I don't believe this was the courier's destination, more like a way station. So, we need to find him and find him fast."

****

It was close to three o'clock and Norm and Arydin were going through the FBI reports coming in from the agents on the ground when suddenly Norm placed a report on the table and started tapping it with his index finger. Arydin could see he was in deep thought and suddenly Norm stood and said, "Let's go visit the local hardware store."

A short time later they stopped in front of a building that had two sections to it. The front of the store carried the type of equipment and supplies you could find in most hardware stores across the country and the back of the building led out into a large lumber yard. Norm and Arydin entered the storefront and heard a female voice call out, offering to help them. As they turned in the direction of the voice, they saw a middle-aged woman walking toward them.

"Yes," Norm replied as he held up his credentials. "We're FBI agents and would like to ask you or whomever owns this business some questions if you don't mind."

The woman introduced herself as Jackie and then she replied, "No I don't mind and will be glad to help if I can but I already had one of your people in here earlier today."

"I know, ma'am, but this is what we call a follow-up with some additional questions."

"Very well, though will you answer a question for me? Is it true that all those Moslems living on the old Gentry farm are dead?"

Norm did not hesitate and his voice portrayed a conspiracy tone, as if telling a secret no one else knew, "Yes, we got all of them."

"Well," Jackie replied, "I am a Christian woman and would see no harm done to any human being but those men gave me the creeps. I don't think they liked having to communicate with women. In my case they didn't have a choice because I am the owner of this business."

Arydin asked, "How did they treat you?"

"It's hard to put in words," she replied. "It's not that they were antisocial, far from it, but they tended to be very secretive and did not attend any of the community projects. And when they came in here to buy something they knew exactly what they wanted. They did not browse around or buy anything they did not have on the list they carried with them. I will say this, they were good customers. They spent a lot of money here and always paid in cash."

"That's what I wanted to talk to you about," Norm replied. "What were their big-ticket items?"

"Well, let's see I think by far it was 6' x 6' posts and 4' x 8' x 2" plywood boards. Also, they ordered several post hole diggers, the large ones and other stuff but you know it's funny that you mention it. Every time they placed an order, we delivered it and unloaded it in their barn. But my driver told me a couple of weeks ago that he never saw anything that they were building with that material. I thought it was strange at the time but then forgot it until now."

Norm asked if they could have an itemized statement of their account and a few moments later she gave it to them. As they were walking out the door she called out, "Oh, by the way they also bought a large backhoe in Pierre shortly after they bought the farm."

****

Norm had placed large sheets of paper on the wall which depicted the supplies and materials purchased by the Moslems and now stood back again in deep thought.

Finally, Arydin said, "Okay Norm, I'm not a farmer. What do you see that I don't?"

Norm pointed to the sheets and answered, "Arydin, those men were supposed to be farmers so why did they buy thousands of 4' X 8' plywood sheets, hundreds of 6' x 8' posts, thousands of feet of electrical wiring, thousands of the 6" venting pipe and," he paused for a second, "a large backhoe?"

"Shit," Arydin said. "They were digging a tunnel."

****

It was close to 6 p.m. and a large group of agents stood beside Norm, Arydin and Agent Protelly at what used to be the farm site.

"All right we're going to start digging from the west side of the building about four feet down and slowly move to the south in a semi-circle. If there's a tunnel out there, we should be able to locate it with the backhoe we borrowed," Agent Protelly said.

Some two hours later they found it. The sun was setting as the group stared down into the hole and they could see where the backhoe had intersected the tunnel. To the right, the tunnel led toward the burned-out farmhouse on the other end it appeared that the tunnel headed south.

As Norm and Arydin started to climb down into the hole, Agent Protelly stopped them by saying, "We don't know what's in that tunnel or how safe it is. My agents will go first and you two can follow."

As the two agents moved into the tunnel, they turned on robust flashlights that penetrated the darkness for one hundred feet or more and now could see the scale of the tunnel. It was four feet wide and six feet deep. The posts, positioned every ten feet, braced the ceiling that was reinforced with plywood. They had wire tacked to the posts and the light bulbs attached. The floor was dirt and muddy.

As the two men worked their way further into the tunnel, Norm was on a secure digital phone talking with General Darwin. When he finished, he turned to Arydin.

"She wants confirmation that we got all of them." Norm said, "and she wants it now."

"Get a doctor over here quick!" Protelly shouted.

Agent Protelly then moved over to them. "The bastards have the tunnel booby-trapped."

"What kind of trap?" Arydin asked.

"They dug a pit in the floor and covered it with a thin sheet of glass and covered that with a couple inches of dirt."

"Did the glass cut him?" Norm asked.

"No, but the bungee sticks they buried tore his legs up pretty bad. His partner is okay but we're going to have to hold still until we can get more people and equipment."

"Can't do that, Agent Protelly. I just had orders to find out where that tunnel goes and what's in it. And I have to find those answers now."

"Well, I'm not sending my agents back into this tunnel until I get some of my Explosive Ordnance Disposal (EOD) people up here."

"Not a problem, Agent Protelly. Arydin and I will go and both of us are trained in explosive ordnance techniques."

"Shit," Protelly replied then said. "OK, if you need to go, two of my agents will go with you and I will be one of them."

****

Arydin was leading the group about forty-five minutes later when he suddenly stopped and dropped down on one knee. "Damn, Norm, we have a problem."

"What's new, Arydin. We already have found two more bungee pits."

"Yes, well this time I think this one's a bomb."

"Christ," Agent Protelly proclaimed, "are you sure?"

Norm moved beside Arydin and saw the thin wire stretched across the tunnel just about two inches above the floor. "How did you spot it, Arydin?" Norm asked.

"Just luck. I saw a glint from the wire as I moved the flashlight."

"So where is the explosive?" Agent Protelly asked.

Arydin slowly moved his hand over the dirt wall and gently removed the dirt where the wire entered the wall. A few seconds passed before they could see the sticks of dynamite inserted in the wall.

"Can you defuse it, Arydin, or do you want me to?" Norm asked.

"Hell no. I found it. I'll do it." He turned to Agent Protelly and said, "Do you and your agent want to go back out of here before I attempt to diffuse the bomb?"

Agent Protelly stated, "What do you mean by attempting to diffuse the bomb? Can you do it? Then get on with it, if not then let's get out of here and I'll have our people do it when they get here."

With that Arydin reached down and pulled the dynamite from the wall.

"Christ!" Agent Protelly shouted. "What the hell are you doing? You could have killed all of us."

"I don't think so," Norm stated. "The wires had to be pulled from the detonator fuse before it exploded. All Arydin did was release the pressure by pulling the dynamite toward the wires."

"That's right," Arydin replied, "but we still have a hot bomb. We can do one of two things, diffuse it now or place the dynamite on the other side of the wall and move on."

"Protelly's explosive ordinance agents can diffuse it later," Norm replied. "I don't want to waste the time."

Protelly turned to the other agent and said, "Guard it but don't touch it. We'll let the EOD team take care of it later."

With that the three of them continued farther into the tunnel. An hour later they reached a sharp turn to the right. They could see a very large room, approximately fifty feet wide, with benches on three sides and a door on the other.

"Well, let's see what we have, but be careful of booby-traps," Norm stated as he moved into the area.

After checking around for several minutes, the three men stood staring at the door in front of them.

"So, what do you think, Agent Protelly?" Norm asked as Arydin moved closer to the door and cautiously started moving his hands over the doorframe.

"I think we have lost the bastard again," he replied angrily. "The evidence we've found points to them having a motorcycle here. And since there's not one here now, I assume it was used to escape when we attacked the farmhouse."

"I agree with you and they were smart about it. It seems from some of the literature we found, they installed some very quiet mufflers on it which probably explains why no one heard it."

"Yes," Arydin replied. "And since we did not find it in the tunnel, he must have left the area through that door. As far as I can determine, it's not booby-trapped. They probably figured if he had to leave in a hurry, they didn't want to take the chance he might detonate an explosive in his attempt to leave. Well, let's hope so."

With that Arydin opened the door. All of them could see the sharp incline and feel the warm breeze entering the tunnel. Seconds later they stood outside in the darkness and the only thing they could see were the lights around the burned-out farmhouse, far in the distance.

"Can you radio some of your people to come out here and pick us up?" Norm asked Agent Protelly. "We can use our flashlights as a beacon."

****

Now back at their boarding room, Arydin paced and deliberated as Norm took a shower. He noticed when Norm came out of the bathroom, he had completely changed his clothes and the ones he had been wearing were now in a large plastic bag with the opening securely taped shut.

Norm looked at Arydin and then said, "Your turn. When you take your clothes off, place them in the bag I left in their first then take the shower. I'll explain when you finish."

Norm was sitting with a cup of coffee in his hands, another cup on the table, and he motioned to it as Arydin set down. A flat brown envelope lay on the center of the table.

Neither man said anything for a few minutes then in a low voice Norm spoke. "Well, my friend I think I've solved part of the plot as to what these people are up to and if I am correct millions of our people could die." He pointed to the envelop. "Inside is a small piece of tape with a miniscule amount of white powder on it. I think it's Anthrax."

"So that's why you were so adamant that only the three of us use one of the cars when we left the site."

"Yes," Norm replied, "and I told Agent Protelly of my concerns when he dropped us off. He will make sure no one goes into that tunnel unless they are fully protected. He should have a team from the Center for Disease Control out of Atlanta on the way up here as we speak. Also, General Darwin has a courier on his way to pick up that envelope and take it to Edgewood Arsenal for testing. I called her while you were in the shower."

"How sure are you of this?" Arydin asked.

Norm shook his head, "Call it a hunch but do you remember that large cabinet next to the wall? It was one of those heavy-duty type. I noticed that they had built a special platform for it to sit on. The cabinet was unlocked and when I opened it there was nothing in it. But dust had settled on the interior and I could clearly see where four round objects had been put on the center shelf.

"I also noticed a very small amount of white powder on the edge of one of the rings. I took a piece of masking tape that I found on one of the benches and used it to pick the powder up. I figured if I am correct from the size of the rings in the dust, they were quart jars, four of them. If they contained Anthrax and are used correctly, they could kill millions of people."

"Why didn't you tell us about it while we were down in the tunnel?" Arydin asked.

"If I'm correct and we're contaminated, it was already too late to do anything about it. My hope is that we are not but, in the morning, we need to have one of the doctors take some blood samples and send them off for testing. Then we will know soon enough. We need to concentrate on finding this guy."

Chapter 11

Two days later, General Darwin stood in front of the conference table facing the two men. It was now 9:15 a.m., June 8, and the meeting had begun in a hostile environment. President Baker at first had declined to come down to the bunker when General Darwin requested the meeting and directed she meet him in the oval office.

She had declined the order and told the chief of staff to tell the president what she had to brief him on was so sensitive that it had to be done in the sensitive compartmented information facility (SCIF) or there would be no meeting and the president might learn about the information from the news media.

The president then had exploded when he learned she would not come to his office and he had yelled at Ed Manson, "Who in the hell does she think is? I'll fire her ass for insubordination."

Ed waited until the president set back down at his desk then said, "Sir, General Darwin would not ask for a meeting in the SCIF if it didn't involve national security. And it must be very important or she would not have decline to brief you in the oval office."

The president had sat brooding for a few moments then said, "All right, Ed, it's now 8 a.m. Tell her we'll go to the SCIF at 9 a.m. Let her sit and wait for a while."

When they arrived in the SCIF, the president sat down and, looking straight at General Darwin, said, "If you ever refuse another one of my orders, I will have you removed from this building. Is that clear? And whatever you have to say had better be important or I may do it now."

Standing ramrod straight Wendy stared hard at the president and it was he who dropped his eyes first.

"Sir, I serve at the pleasure of the president, no matter who that individual may be. If it is your desire to have me replaced, I will contact the Department of Defense and request a transfer."

The president did not answer but Wendy observed the flush that crept across his face.

Ed Manson broke the impasse by asking, "General Darwin, what's this meeting about?"

As if talking to an invisible person she requested the situation board be activated. Immediately the display appeared in front of them. With the laser pointer she highlighted the next to last item in the list and the president's head shot up.

"Congressman Frank Wolk called me at 5:22 this morning requesting information on an incident in his district that happened yesterday. As you know he serves on the powerful Armed Services committee, in fact he chairs it. I told him that either you, Mr. President, or I would get back to him as soon as we could verify the information we have.

"I know he's from the opposition party but he has been a close ally of mine for many years and one that can be trusted with the information if we brief him on the situation that's currently on-going."

With that said, she briefed the two men on what happened at the farmhouse in South Dakota.

The president moved swiftly to his feet when she told him about the Anthrax threat and in a shaky voice ask, "Is that true?"

"Yes, Sir, I'm afraid it is," she replied. "The sample Lieutenant Norm Shepherd sent was tested in a lab at Fort Dietrich this morning and the test results came back as weapons grade. Right now, my subordinates think there are four quarts of it out there someplace."

"Do we have any idea where it came from?" Ed Manson asked.

"No, but we have a theory. Before the second Iraq War, the UN inspectors team reported that Iraq had hundreds of liters of Anthrax. During and afterwards, we never found or uncovered any. It was believed that it had been shipped out to another country in the region just prior to the start of the invasion. But that was never proven. I will know in the next twenty-four hours if it is the Anthrax that the UN inspectors found in Iraq."

Again, the chief of staff asked, "How sure are we that this courier or whatever he is has the stuff?"

"Well, first we know from the residue left in that tunnel that it was there and we also know it's not there now. We know the fugitive left on a motorcycle as soon as the FBI raided the farmhouse. We also know the bike had been modified with heavy-duty mufflers to reduce the noise. In addition, our agents found a catalog and cash receipt for the bike saddlebags. A picture of one had been circled in the brochure. if it was the one used it could easily hold four-quart size containers. Our people are checking with the company which sells them and we should soon know if these people purchased one but I believe they did."

In an infuriated voice, the president wailed, "What are we going to do? We must find these people before they attack us. Christ, it cannot be that hard to find one man on a motorcycle. Do something and do it now General Darwin. I put you in charge of this situation and if you fail it will be on your head and not mine." With that he stood and left the room.

General Darwin turned to Ed, shook her head and then said, "You can tell him we have every FBI agent in the country looking for him and at 6 a.m. this morning I ordered two divisions of the 101st Airborne to drop into not only South Dakota but the surrounding states. That includes North Dakota, Iowa, Wyoming and Nebraska. Their task is to cover every road in those states at strategic locations. They should be dropping into those areas within the hour."

The chief of staff stood and begin pacing. "I don't believe you should have done that without the president's approval, General Darwin."

"I was going to tell him but he didn't give me the time to do so. You tell him, Mr. Manson, and he can call it off if he wishes. But it's the quickest way that I know to seal off that area before we lose that man again."

"Hell," Ed replied, "there's no way we can hide something that large from the public. It will be all over the news within minutes after they leave the aircrafts."

"I know that, Ed, but to give us some time I had the Department of Defense prepare a news release stating that President Baker had ordered a major exercise code-named 'Cold Wind' be conducted today. Here's a copy of the release. Give it to him. He can either sign it for release or come up with another explanation or, as I said, he can cancel the airborne drop.

"Just remember this, Mr. Manson, those states are not heavily populated and with enough manpower guarding the roads I think we have a good chance of catching him if he's driving on them. If he has gone to ground and is hole-up somewhere we can start a massive house search. It's the best I could come up with for the time being. Now I have one final question. What does the president want to do about Congressman's Frank Wolk's request?"

"I'll get back to you with an answer as soon as I can," he answered as he left the room.

Wendy went over and poured a cup of coffee. She was thinking that the president did not even ask the status of my two operatives or the FBI agents who fought and some died at the farmhouse.

Chapter 12

It was 9:15 a.m. as Lieutenant Shepherd with Lieutenant Hassan at his side watched the parachutes glide down from the sky. There seem to be hundreds of them and what a beautiful sight it was.

All over the four states that scene was repeated as the paratroopers moved to their designated target areas. Their assignments were to cover all the crossroads in that specific area. When local citizens approached the soldiers, they could see that they were in combat gear and heavily loaded with weapons. When they asked what was happening the reply was always the same, the president had directed a major exercise to be conducted in the area. And it seemed to satisfy them since the soldiers took no proactive actions. They just setup bivouac areas and sat beside the roads. The people even thought it was exciting when their vehicles were pulled over, checked and immediately released to continue on their way. The public thought they were part of the exercise.

Agent Protelly drove up and as he got out of his vehicle he pointed to the sky and shouted, "You men want to explain that?"

Arydin chuckled and stated, "I think your guys just got some help."

****

Some twenty minutes later Norm, Arydin, Agent Protelly and one other man in full combat gear sat together in the FBI command post. The new man was a general with two stars on his helmet and commanded the paratroopers.

"All right does anyone want to explain why I had to airdrop sixteen thousand paratroops out all over God's creation to watch roads?" he asked. Then he continued, "I hope you have a good answer, Lieutenant Hassan, because I have been directed from higher authority to follow your orders to the letter. I think that is a little unorthodox since I was taught there is a chain of command and as far as I know it's always been from the top down not the other way around."

Lieutenant Hassan thought to himself, thanks General Darwin.

Norm just smiled to himself. Norm had told Arydin that General Darwin had ordered two divisions of paratroopers to cover not only South Dakota but the surrounding states as well. Their sole purpose was to ensure that if the courier attempted to use the roads by any means he was to be captured or killed.

After Arydin finish briefing the general, the general stood and walked across the room to the wall map and placed his finger over the city of Winner. Looking back at the three men he stated, "Now I know why General Darwin directed all my troops carry Anthrax filters for their mask but what's the special unit of Rangers that landed with me supposed to do?"

Arydin rose and joined him at the map. He drew a circle around the town of Winner then asked, "How many personnel do you have in that group, General?"

"Five-hundred," the general replied.

"Very well. Have those people set up a cordon some twenty miles outside the city and once that is done slowly start moving them inward toward the town. We don't think the man could have gotten very far on that motorcycle and he may have another safe house close by. It's a long shot but we need to know if he is already long gone. They will need to check every house, barn, shed or any other place one could hide."

Agent Protelly spoke, "Are you telling me the military is now in control?"

Norm answered, "No, your people as the civilian representatives of the government has jurisdiction over this matter. The military is here to assist you and they will take their orders through the military chain of command which is Lieutenant Hassan. That is until such time as the president decides to declare martial law. If that should happen the military could assume command of the situation."

The general said, "Well, gentlemen until the president enacts the Posse Comitatus Act, which he has not done to my knowledge as of now, we do not have the authority to trespass on private property. By that I mean the Army, Air Force, Navy and the Marine Corps.

"The law was enacted in 1878 and if my memory has not failed me it states, "Whoever, except in cases and under circumstances expressly authorized by the Constitution or Act of Congress, willfully uses any part of the Army or Air Force as a posse comitatus or otherwise to execute the laws shall be fined under this title or imprisoned not more than two years, or both."

"Gentlemen, I hope you understand what you are asking of me and I for one will tell you I do not intend to go to prison nor for that matter any of my men," stated the general.

"Sir, I hope it does not have to come to that," Norm replied. "Although we have not had the opportunity to discuss this with Agent Protelly, we want him to supply us with agents that can be embedded with your troops. That way they can handle the legal issues and leave your men to conduct the search."

Norm asked, "Can you do that Protelly?"

At first, he thought the agent would balk at the request but Protelly answered, "Tell me how many people you want and I will have them here in thirty minutes."

After the two men left Arydin said, "Norm, I don't think either one of them are very happy. I sure know the general is not. Did you know General Darwin was putting me in control of the military assets?"

"Not at first," Norm replied, "but I am glad I'm not the one between Protelly and the general. Let's go find something to eat and figure out what we need to do next."

Chapter 13

It was close to two o'clock when General Darwin pulled up to the coffee shop in D.C. not far from the Capitol building and watched as the man came out the door and entered her vehicle.

Without saying anything she pulled back into the traffic. She looked into her rearview mirror and could not determine if she was being tailed but that did not mean anything. She knew if she was followed, they would be good and she probably would not spot them anyway, especially if they were Secret Service agents.

Neither of them spoke until they reached their destination, the grassy knoll just below the graves at The Arlington National Cemetery. Wendy got out of the car then turned to the man now standing beside her. "Frank, thank you for coming."

Congressman Frank Wolk smiled and replied, "The pleasure is mine, Wendy." Then he pointed to the gravesite. "You know I come here on occasion not as often as I would like but two of them as you know were close friends."

As they walked up the knoll, they both saw the young female Marine standing at parade rest. As they neared the graveside the young Marine slowly came to attention and her right hand came to her hat in a rigid salute.

Congressman Wolk was startled for a second then saw Wendy return the salute and drop her hand. The Marine did as well but she remained at attention.

The congressman turned to her, "Wendy, I never saw any of the Marine guards do that before and I have been here when other military brass was here as well. Those soldiers always stayed at parade rest. Have new procedures been instituted?"

"I don't know, Frank. Until a couple of days ago I had never seen it done either."

Then they both observed a male Marine colonel in full dress uniform move down the slope toward them. As he approached, the colonel saluted Wendy and said, "Good afternoon, General Darwin. May I intrude for a moment and speak frankly?"

Wendy nodded yes and noticed the Marine guard was still standing at a rigid attention but she had not saluted the officer as he approached.

"I am sure you are not aware of this, Ma'am, but you started a revolt within the Corps a few days ago."

"What do you mean, Colonel?" she asked.

He then told her the story of the salute to her and how it had raged within the Corps on returning the salute to her as she left the graveside.

"Those past and present who have served as guards for this site have taken it upon themselves to give you the honor you deserve and as of today those rules have been accepted by all the Corps. I might add, that it's been a long time coming."

Wendy was stunned and did not know what to say but she could feel the pride swell within her. Then she asked, "What happened to the Marine guard who first saluted me?"

The colonel hesitated for a second then stated, "Sergeant Dotson is in the brig awaiting a court martial for not following orders Ma'am."

The colonel was not sure how General Darwin was going to react to that but was surprised when he saw the smile spread across her face. Then he heard words that just added to her legend.

"Colonel, I want orders cut immediately for Sergeant Dotson. I want him transferred to my staff and I want him in my office by 6 p.m. tonight."

"Yes, Ma'am," he replied, saluted, turned and left.

The young Marine guard remained at attention but they could see the smile on her face. A few minutes later as they turned to leave, the guard returned Wendy's salute and then went back to parade rest.

As they both got into the car Frank said, "That's the damnedest thing I ever saw but I agree with the colonel you deserve it. Now what do you want to talk about?"

After briefing him he sat there in stunned disbelief. "My God, Wendy, what does the president think he's doing? The country is in grave danger and he's sitting there in the Oval Office hiding."

"I don't know, Frank, but if for any reason I have to leave the White House someone other than his people need to know the truth."

"Hell, Wendy, he can't fire you. It would cause a national uproar."

"Uproars die down, Frank, but you know he has been stonewalling your request for information and I doubt he will provide any."

"What are you going to tell him about our meeting?"

"The truth if he asked," she replied, "but I will also tell him you have given me your word not to go public with the information at this time. Frank, I need time to see if we can catch these people before they can strike this country. If it looks like we can't then take whatever action you think best."

****

At 6 p.m., Sergeant Dotson was standing at attention in front of General Darwin's desk.

Chapter 14

It was not too long after Harris had left the farmhouse that he saw the lights from the explosion that destroyed the farmhouse but by then he was well on his way to his next destination. When he arrived, he saw the small aircraft already waiting on the dirt airstrip and a man standing by the hangar motioning him to enter.

As Harris drove the bike into the hangar, the man closed the door and turned to him, "We must hurry if we are to escape." With that he turned and started toward the aircraft. Harris followed.

Once in the aircraft the pilot explained they would only be in the air for a short time before they reached their next destination.

The two men had been waiting at the landing strip for the aircraft's arrival and turned on the runway lights when the cell phone rang. They did not attempt to answer but knew that was their signal that the aircraft was only a few minutes from its destination. As soon as the aircraft landed, they opened the hangar doors and quickly closed them after the aircraft taxied in.

The lights inside were bright and when Harris stepped out of the aircraft he carried the saddle bags. He carefully placed them on a work bench located along one of the walls and removed two of the quart jars.

He was nervous both because he had never flown before let alone at night but his encounter at the farmhouse in Winner had been too close. He couldn't understand how the authorities had found him so soon and knew it had been only luck and Allah's will that he had escaped.

He turned and looked at the two men standing beside the small aircraft. Both men were in their mid-twenties. One was of Asian heritage and the other Caucasian.

Harris addressed the men, "Do you have the containers?"

Each man held out a bag that looked like a carrying case for a water bottle. In fact, that is what they were, well insulated with the Velcro covers. They were the type hunters and backpackers would use and were so common no one would pay any attention to them.

A few minutes later each man had one of the quart jars tucked inside and without a word headed for the second light aircraft. The two men were airborne and gone in a short period of time.

Harris and his pilot refueled their aircraft from fifty-gallon drums of fuel stored in the hangar and when they finished Harris asked, "What about the people who live here?"

The pilot shook his head, "I don't know. The two who just left took care of that problem."

****

Harris looked at his watch, 3:50 a.m., June 8, then took the saddlebags from the bench and headed for the aircraft.

The pilot taxied the aircraft outside, stopped and returned to the hangar, shutting off the lights and closing the hangar doors. A few minutes later they were airborne.

****

It was close to 9 a.m. as Norm and Arydin listened to Protelly brief them on the actions taken place over the past twenty-four hours. It had been a long night and neither man had much sleep on the aircraft on their return to Winner, South Dakota after their meeting with General Darwin in Washington.

Protelly was angry and they could hear the frustration in his voice as he stated, "You both know the courier got away by either flying a small aircraft from a farm a few miles from here or by having someone fly him out of here. From what we have found out so far, it's more than likely he had an accomplice. The farm couple who owned the aircraft kept it on their property and flew it off on a dirt runway. We also found out that a few months ago they had hired someone to help with the spring planting and provided room and board for him. But we do not have much of a description for him but he appeared to be in his late twenties or early thirties, light complexion, brown hair and a short beard.

"Since the farm couple are dead from gunshot wounds and he has not been found he probably is the pilot. We have our people going over that farm with a fine-tooth comb and if the individual is an American, we should be able to identify him. He could not have stayed on that farm as long as he did without leaving fingerprints.

"But that's not the worst of it. About twenty minutes ago your Rangers and two of my men were working an area around Presho, South Dakota about thirty-five miles from here. They discovered a farm couple murdered by gun shots in their home. The deaths had occurred sometime within the past twenty-four hours. They also had a small landing field, hangar and one aircraft. Again, they had hired two men to help with their spring planting in the past few weeks. At this point we have a very limited description of them; one was Asian and the other was Caucasian. Neither man has been found and the farmer's aircraft is missing."

Norm spoke, "Where do you think they will link up? They will have to rendezvous with the courier someplace."

"We are already too late for that," Protelly stated. "Your Rangers are good at what they do. They were able, with the dew on the ground, to determine that within the past few hours a plane had landed on that strip and two aircraft had taken off. The courier was there and now they're all gone."

"Damn!" Norm stated, standing up and leaving the room.

Arydin asked Protelly, "What are you doing to try and trace them?"

"First since we know they can cover at least four hundred miles before they must land, if not for any other reason than to refuel. I am having every agent I can start checking four hundred miles out from Presno, South Dakota in a 360° arc starting at the outer perimeter and working inward. Primary areas of concern are farm strips, then local airstrips and finally commercial airports.

"Second, I have asked FBI headquarters to request all noncommercial aircraft in that area to be grounded immediately. I don't know how that will go over with FAA since they have no idea why that needs to be done."

"Thanks, Protelly," Arydin responded and stood up. "I will cancel the exercise. No need for them to sit out on those roads now but I will keep the Rangers going. They might find something you never know." and he left.

He found Norm outside leaning against the car staring at the sky as if in a trance but Arydin knew better. It was a trait Norm had when he was in deep thought.

Finally, Norm looked at him and said, "Arydin, I'm concerned we're not going to find them before they can attack and if that is the case then we need to figure out how they are going to do it. We know what they intend to use, so how are they going to accomplish it and more important when? We're not doing any good here so it's time to return to Washington and I want Protelly to go with us. You want to tell him, or should I?"

Arydin grinned, "I think he likes you better than me. You do it," and he turned and headed for the car.

****

They had been in the air for less than an hour when the aircraft suddenly banked to the left and was soon heading back the way they had come.

They then heard the pilot state, "General Darwin has directed we change course and proceed to Miles City, Montana. It seems the Montana civil air patrol has located a small aircraft that has crashed near Broadus Montana. Miles City has an airport that can accommodate this aircraft and the air guard out of Billings, Montana is sending two helicopters and a hazmat team to that location."

Protelly replaced the cell phone in his pocket. "That was my operations center. That aircraft is believed to be the one missing from Presho, South Dakota. It's down in a desolate area about forty miles north of Broadus, Montana. The civil air patrol spotters stated there was no fire. It appears the aircraft nosed straight in and there are no survivors."

"Is there any place near the accident site that they could have landed?" Norm asked?

"No," Protelly answered. They were given explicit orders to stay away from the aircraft."

Norm walked up to the pilot's cabin and asked if they had any maps of eastern Montana and wind directions in that area. A few minutes later the three men were studying a map of the area.

"We're lucky in one-way," Arydin stated. "If that aircraft was carrying any of the Anthrax and it scattered upon impact, there is nothing out there but prairie and small hills."

"You may be right, Arydin, but the surface winds in that area are a steady ten to fifteen miles an hour and in an easterly direction. If the wind carries that stuff, at some point people are going to encounter it."

****

Twenty minutes later, President Baker finished reading the report General Darwin had sent him by way of Ed Manson. He laid the paper on his desk and Ed could see he was scared, really scared. Yet, he did not say anything. It was almost as if he was frozen in a trance.

Finally, Ed said, "Mr. President, we are not going to keep the lid on this much longer. General Darwin is correct. With that downed aircraft and the five hundred Rangers she redeployed to cordon off that accident site, the news media, not to mention Congressman Wolk whom you have not briefed yet, will be clamoring for answers."

"Do we know for sure that aircraft was carrying any of that Anthrax?" the president ask.

"No, Sir, and we will not know until that Air Force hazmat team from Billings can reach the site or the monitors the Rangers are carrying can detect any airborne samples of the stuff."

"Very well, Ed. Contact the major news outlets and tell them I intend to hold a major news conference in thirty minutes. If General Darwin cannot contain this situation, I will."

"Very good, Sir. Do you want me to write a script for you?"

"No, I will take care of that myself."

****

Thirty minutes later, the president stood before the White House press corps. They all sat in stunned silence as the president told them and the nation of the threat they now faced.

Finally, he stated, "I had General Darwin in charge of finding these people and eliminating this threat and I am sorry to say she has failed. As of now she is being relieved of her command and reassigned to the Pentagon."

The uproar lasted for several minutes before he could speak again and then he said, "I have sent a request to congress for Martial law until this situation can be resolved. And I have ordered our military command to start rounding up all Moslems in this country and hold them in detention camps until they can be deported to their countries of origin."

The press corps had no opportunity to ask questions. The president had turned and left the podium.

Ed Manson was in stunned silence as the president walked by and thought, all hell is going to break loose.

Chapter 15

The staff on duty in the conference room could see the flush raise on General Darwin face as she sat watching the president tell the nation that she was relieved of duty. It had not surprised her but he could have told her prior to announcing it to the world.

She left the room and walked down the hall to her office where she found Ed Manson waiting for her. She could see the man's discomfort and she smiled.

"All right, Ed, are you here to escort me out of the building?"

Ed shook his head. "No, General Darwin. I wanted you to know that I nor anyone else in the White House had any idea what the president was going to say. He wrote the speech himself. He must be out of his mind. It's bad enough that the country is in turmoil but we now have a revolt going on in the White House."

"What do you mean, Ed?"

Most of the staff is resigning their positions in droves in protest over reassigning you."

"They should not do that, Ed. The country needs a strong government in this crisis not a divided one."

"I agree, General Darwin, but as smart as you are you have a flaw and that is you do not realize how loved you are by the American people. You symbolize what the people expect from its government. You just don't realize the power you have but you are the only person who can and must do something to get us out of this crisis."

She looked thoughtful at him for a moment then said, "I will prepare a letter for the staff which may stop this nonsense. You will have it in an hour." She then walked to her desk and pulled two envelopes out of the drawer. She handed one to Ed and he could see it was addressed to the president.

"That it is my letter of resignation. The other is for the joint chiefs of staff notifying them of my retirement from military service effective immediately."

"God, you can't do that, General Darwin," Ed cried.

"Yes, I can and it is not something I am doing on the spur of the moment. I have been thinking about it for some time now and the letters have been in my desk for the past couple of weeks. There is another reason why now the time is to go. If I stayed, the unrest would just continue to fester. There's that old saying out-of-sight out-of-mind and with me out of the picture things should die down rather quickly, at least I hope so."

"There is one thing you can do for me, Ed, or at least try."

"If I can I will," Ed replied.

"I don't believe what the president is doing is legal or constitutional in regard to interning and deporting all the Moslems in the country but that will have to be sorted out by congress and the supreme court. I am concerned about one of my staff. Lieutenant Arydin is a Moslem. Can you see if the president will give him a pass on internment until the legal issues have been resolved?"

"I will do my best, Ma'am."

With that Ed left her office and forty-five minutes later he had the letter she had promised to write. Within minutes the content was all over the government and the nation as well because it had been leaked to the press.

It simply addressed the government employees of the United States.

> My fellow countrymen, in times of great threats to this country it is you who must bear the most burden in a crisis. Our political leadership and military personnel will, as they have always done, act to defend and protect our nation, but it will be accomplished through you.
>
> You are the backbone of the government and it is your efforts that ensure it is accomplished and now is another threat that you must face. Do your best. It's what the citizens of our country expect. We will prevail.
>
> General Wendy Darwin, June 8, 2040

Chapter 16

The country was gripped in fear and demanding that the government take action to prevent another terrorist attack on the country and President Baker's firing of Lieutenant General Darwin had caused a firestorm of protest from the American public. Many in congress were demanding President Baker be impeached and that call was coming from both sides of the aisle.

As Congressman Wolk sat in the house chamber listening to the debate raging around him, a page suddenly appeared and stated, "General Darwin wishes to speak with you."

"Where is she?" he asked.

"In your office."

"Tell her I will be right there."

****

Frank had been surprised to learn Wendy was in his office and when he arrived, he found her standing next to his desk. He was struck by the fact she was in civilian attire. He tried to think back to when he had seen her out of uniform and he could not.

As usual she had come right to the point and stated she would like to work for him but only until the current crisis was over and without pay. He had been stunned and at first did not know what to say. Wendy had continued and stated she had an agenda and felt congress was the best place to pursue it. She did not tell him what it was but simply stated I work cheap.

Frank had thrown up his hands, "Hell, Wendy you can have my office if you want."

"That won't be necessary, Frank, but I would appreciate it if you could find an office where I can work in private."

****

At 4 p.m. a press release was issued from Congressman Frank Wolk's office which was reported on all the national news organizations within minutes. It simply stated that retired Lieutenant General Wendy Darwin would join his staff effective tomorrow morning.

****

Ed Manson had watched as President Baker learned that Wendy had become an aide on Congressman Wolk's staff. He had gone into a fit of rage but Ed could see the fear in his eyes. He knew he had gone too far when he fired Wendy but had been unprepared for the onslaught of protest from both the civilian and military communities. He could only hope it would die down as time passed but a part of the him knew it would not and he could lose the presidency.

****

Norm and Arydin had listened in disbelief on what was going on in Washington. Arydin had become strangely quiet when they heard that all Moslems in the country were to be rounded up and deported. It didn't help that they were standing on the prairie a short distance from the crash site surrounded by some fifteen to twenty air National Guard personnel who were now staring at Arydin, some with hostility in their eyes. If Arydin noticed, he did not show it.

It was close to 3 p.m. when they saw two of the survey teams in yellow one-piece suits and oxygen masks move toward them. One was carrying a small metal container. He suddenly stopped and laid the container on the ground and the other continued walking until he reached Norm. He had one of the detectors the CDC had provided them and pointed to it.

"We could find no trace of Anthrax in the area but we did find that metal container in the wreckage. It's banged up but appears to be intact. The Anthrax, if there is any, may be in that container. Do you want us to attempt to open it?"

"No," Norm replied. "We need to obtain an air-tight carrier and then have it delivered to Edgewood Arsenal. I will take care of that."

Norm turned to Protelly who had been standing by listening to the conversation. "Protelly, can you have three or four of your agents guard that container until we're ready to move it?"

"Yes," he replied and reached for his cell phone.

Norm thanked the man, turned back to his partner and both of them left the area, leaving the container out on the prairie.

****

Three hours later the container had been placed inside another container and was in the cargo hold of the aircraft taking Norm, Arydin and Protelly back to Washington.

Norm and Arydin were pondering the critical message they had received from Wendy.

"Upon arrival in Washington have Agent Protelly deliver the container to Edgewood Arsenal. They will be waiting for him at the main gate. Both of you leave the aircraft as soon as it lands, talk to no one and meet me at the place I am most comfortable."

When Norm told Protelly of the arrangement for he and his agents to take the container to Edgewood he balked and stated, "I am not taking that box anyplace without higher authority. General Darwin is now no longer in a position of authority or in charge of this mission." With that he moved to the back of the plane. He stayed back there for about ten minutes and then returned to his seat.

"Well, he stated, "she may not be in charge anymore but you could not tell it by me. The director said I was to follow her instructions to the letter and to stand by to support both of you until this crisis is over."

Norm just shook his head but did not say anything. Arydin had his eyes closed but Norm was not sure if he was asleep or not.

As Norm and Arydin left the plane, a woman in civilian clothing met them with instructions to pick up a red Ford Taurus in the parking lot. Then she handed Norm a set of keys, turned and left. A few minutes later both men were in the car and driving into Washington.

Arydin asked, "Norm do you know where we're to meet General Darwin?"

"Yes, I know exactly where she wants us to meet. We're going to my mother's house."

Chapter 17

The courier asked the pilot, "How far is it to the next safe house?"

The man replied, "I have orders to fly you just outside of Iowa Falls, Iowa. We should arrive in about thirty minutes. Like the last one our people took control of it yesterday, we will only be on the ground a short period of time, just long enough to refuel then I'm to fly you to another farm near Yates City, Illinois which again our people will be waiting for you." The man hesitated for a second and then continued, "Our people will make it look like a robbery had occurred and their plane will remain in their hangar. I will refuel and fly back to Iowa and turn north to lure anyone who may be tracking us away from this area."

"Where do you intend to land?" the courier asked.

The pilot smiled as he answered, "Into the biggest building I can find before I run out of gas." Then he shouted, "Allah is Great."

It was early afternoon when the aircraft landed on the dirt strip near Yates City.

****

Norm's mother had been surprised when her son and Arydin arrived but was delighted. She made supper for them before she finally asked, "OK, what's going on?"

Norm knew not to lie to her, he never could. So, he told her about the cryptic note Wendy had sent him.

She stood looking at the two men then smiled, "I think you may be right, Norm, so I had better go make a fresh pot of coffee."

An hour later, Wendy arrived and as she entered the kitchen both men rose from their chairs.

She flashed a small smile and she said, "Since I am no longer in military service there is no need to stand at attention in my presence," and she motioned them to sit.

She then poured herself a cup of coffee and sat down facing them. "Norm, I asked your mother if I could speak with both of you in private and she

71

graciously consented and has retired to her room. Your mother also asked if I would like to stay here until this crisis is over and I have accepted her invitation. I will be using the spare bedroom for some electronic and communication equipment arriving tomorrow and I will need your bedroom so box up anything you want and put it in your closet."

"Yes, Ma'am," Norm replied and saw a smile creep across Arydin face.

Wendy saw it as well and turned to face him. "Arydin, it must be extremely difficult for you under the present circumstances but you must remain focused on the task at hand. I don't believe the president's mandate to deport all Moslems will come to pass but if the terrorists do strike it may very well happen. I had asked the president to give you a waiver for detainment until this crisis is over. He said no but did consent to give you seventy-two hours before you would have to report to a detention center. If it comes to that I will fight it with all the power I have. So, you and Norm have seventy-two hours to resolve this crisis and that means no attack on this country.

"Now here is what I want you to do."

****

Norm and Arydin left the house at 7 a.m. the next morning and by 7:30 they were having breakfast in a small diner in downtown Washington, DC with Nick Protelly.

Nick put his coffee cup down and shook his head. "I have been placed into a position that I cannot believe is happening. The director has made me a conduit for every federal agency and military infrastructure for the two of you and your orders no matter what they are will be carried out to the letter."

"Damn!" Protelly said. "Only the president has that power or at least that's what I was taught to believe. On top of that, he is effectively being left out of the loop except for any reports you two send him. I have never been comfortable with you two since this crisis started six days ago but I have a feeling that I would be transferred to Butte Montana if I was even hesitant about supporting you and I definitely don't want to go to Butte Montana."

"Why, what's so bad about Butte Montana?" Arydin asked.

Norm answered, "It's what FBI agents call purgatory. It started back in the nineteen forties or fifties or so an FBI agent told me a few years ago. Butte,

Montana is a copper mining town and over the years the mining pit has become one of the largest holes in the country. It got larger and larger until the lip of the crater reached the edge of town.

"Agents sent there are left completely out of the system. They're given an office with a desk and left to their minor duties. That all stopped in the early nineties but FBI agents have never forgotten it."

"Oh," was all Arydin said and Protelly said nothing.

"So where are we at now?" Norm asked.

"It's not good," Protelly stated. "First Edgewood tested that material in the canister and it is Anthrax in pure form which could, if used right, kill hundreds of thousands of people. We also believe we know where it came from. It's not American-made and homeland security believes it may have come from the Middle East within the past six months and probably through the West Coast. Los Angeles to be exact. It seems a small local hospital had a patient six months ago who came in with symptoms that the hospital staff could not identify and the man died the next day. His wife had the body removed for burial at a local cemetery.

"As you know our people have been back tracking looking for anything unusual and this incident caught the eye of one of our agents. Three days ago, when he interviewed the wife, he learned that the husband was a sailor and his ship had just returned from a trip to the Middle East and the man was a Moslem. Yesterday, they got a court order and exhumed the body. It did not take long to determine the man died from Anthrax and it was the same kind we have at Edgewood.

"All the people who lived in that area have been detained and questioned as we speak but I don't think we will find much. The man more than likely turned over the Anthrax to someone as soon as he left the ship."

"What makes you think that?" Norm asked.

"Well, the man somehow infected himself with a strong enough dose that he died within a day of arriving. If he took the stuff home it would seem others would be infected as well but to date no one has, as far as we can tell.

"We also think the individual who he passed the stuff to transported it to the farmhouse in Winner, South Dakota. He, more than likely, hid it on that farm, when the Norton's employed him, and was the pilot who flew the courier out of there. It's all conjecture right now but it fits the pattern were starting to

73

see. It also tells us the terrorist group is larger than we thought and that scares me.

"The second plane carrying the courier has not been found but this morning there was apparently murder and robbery of a farm couple near the small town of Iowa Falls. The farmer had a dirt runway and hanger but the plane was still there, even though they had ransacked the house.

"When the local authorities started questioning the neighbors if they had noticed anything unusual in the area one mentioned he had seen a small aircraft land on that strip earlier this morning and take off a few minutes later. The authorities contacted our local field office and our people are at the scene now."

"What makes you think it's our man?" Norm asked.

"Well, you both know when those two planes left South Dakota they had a range of approximately four hundred miles on a tank of gas. We know what happened to one plane but the other plane that we think the courier is on would have put him at the outer limits of Iowa Falls.

"I don't think that was a robbery at that farmhouse. I think they were after gas to refuel their plane. It fits with the aircraft that landed and left a short time later. Our people are checking to find out how much fuel was store on that farm.

"This group whoever they are have planned all this in a minute detail and it's not something they have done on short notice. Their action for moving the courier at least for the present is by air and they have up until now targeted farmers who have local airstrips and aircraft.

"I have moved our area of search to Iowa Falls, again using that four-hundred-mile grid. We're conducting a search through FAA records to identify all local pilots in that area. Those who identify their occupation as farmers are flagged and I have two-man teams deploying to those farms. If they continue to use that mode of operation, sooner or later our people will be there to meet them.

"One last thing, based on the flight path of that plane it appears the courier is heading east."

"I think you're right, Protelly, and I believe your assumptions are correct," Norm replied, "and I know one way we can bring him back to ground. I want you to contact the FAA and instruct them to ground all small noncommercial aircraft."

"What? You can't do that!" Protelly exclaimed.

"Yes, I can," Norm replied, just give them this phone number for verification and authority to do just that. And I want that order accomplished within the next two hours."

Protelly just looked at him for a few seconds and then stood and left the room.

Arydin looked at Norm, "I don't think he likes you very much either," and pointed to the plates on the table. "He left the bill for you to pay."

"We need Protelly and so I don't want to push him too hard. If we are going to catch this guy he will play a key role in it. Let's go. We have a lot of work to do."

Chapter 18

The pilot took his headset off and turned to the courier, "I just received a message from the control tower at O'Hare International Airport. FAA has directed the grounding of all small aircraft across the country immediately. All aircraft in the air are to land at the nearest airport," and he hesitated for a second then continued, "any aircraft that does not comply will be intercepted and shot down."

"Can we make it to our destination?" the courier asked.

"I believe so," he replied, "but it will be close. We still have an hour to go and if we are not targeted by radar or a military aircraft we should make it to Yates City, Illinois."

"Do what you have to. Just get there or all we have worked for will be lost."

Some forty-five minutes later, the pilot announced, "We have been targeted. O'Hare controllers are demanding we land at Yates City. If I don't, they will intercept us with military aircraft even though our destination is thirty minutes from Yates City. If I do not respond and land there, they will know who we are."

"We must not land at Yates City," the courier replied.

"I know," the pilot said. "Here is what I intend to do. I will declare an in-flight emergency and drop down to treetop level, land at the farm strip just long enough for you to deplane, then take off and head for Yates City. Once there I will crash the plane into a building. Hopefully they will think it's just an accident and give you time to escape."

The courier grabbed the pilot's arm and said, "Allah be with you. You will not be forgotten."

Some ten minutes later the control tower operator at Yates City had the small aircraft insight then watched in horror as the plane suddenly veered to the right and crashed into a hangar. But the pilot made a mistake. The controller suddenly reached over and rewound the tape and replayed the last two minutes of the conversation he had with the pilot. Right at the end of the tape, he heard it again. The pilot's last words were "Allah is great". The controller reached for the phone.

Chapter 19

By 6 a.m., long before most staffers came to work, Wendy arrived at her new office in the Capitol building. However, word had spread rapidly where her office was and everyone who could wanted a chance to see her.

The hall was full of staffers when she arrived and though no one said anything they all started clapping as she walked to her office. It took her by surprise and a faint flush moved across her face but she turned and faced the them before going through the door and said thank you.

When Congressman Wolk heard about the incident, he picked up the phone and a few minutes later two of the capitol police guards were standing outside of her door and two more were at each end of the corridor. He wanted to make sure she had the privacy that she had asked for and for some uneasy reason he also wanted to provide some protection for her as well.

He could not believe anyone would want to harm her but he was not about to take any chances. He picked up the phone and about four hours later sat in his conference room looking at the twelve men and women seated at the table. Every one of them were retired Navy Seals, FBI agents, military personnel or Secret Service personnel.

"First," he stated, "I would like to thank you all for coming and second what I say to you must remain between us. If you cannot abide by that you can leave now." No one moved.

"Very well. What I am going to ask you to do has no backing of the United States government. I will pay for expenses incurred from my own pocket but all of you will have to volunteer with no pay to support this mission."

Again no one said anything but all were wondering where this was going.

"Most of you in this group have at one time or another crossed path with the others and all have been exceptional in your career or field."

"What is it you want us to do?" one of the women asked.

Congressman Wolk looked at her and stated, "I want all of you to set up a security team that will provide protection for Ms. Wendy Darwin," and he paused, "and I don't want her to know about it."

The group was stunned at what they had just heard and then one of the men stood and stated, "Congressman Wolk, I don't think anyone in this group would not be honored to provide what you are asking for but I do have a question. If the general's life may be in danger, and I will continue to call her general, then I for one feel we need a larger contingent of personnel to do the job right." He waved his hand to those sitting there and said, "Each of these individuals have resources and friends they worked with for years, some retired others not, but if each of us could pull in five more individuals we would have a sixty-person team in place within a day or two. Those who would join us would abide by the same set of rules we will honor."

The congressman looked at them and said, "So be it."

As they started to stand the man who had been talking continued, "And by the way, Congressman Wolk, there will be no cost to you or the government. We will take care of it."

****

Twenty-four hours later, Secret Service agent John Wills sat in Congressman Wolk's office briefing him on the new security team they had established to protect General Darwin.

Frank could hardly believe what he was hearing, within twenty-four hours they had twelve teams in place and General Darwin was already under protection when she left the Capitol last night.

When the congressman had asked where the command center was, the man had replied that it was located over in the Secret Service vehicle garage on Ninth Street. "It's perfect for our mission, it's secure, has office space on the second floor and communication assets already in place."

"But what will happen if the Secret Service director finds out you have a clandestine operation going on in his building?"

The man smiled and replied, "Sir, the Secret Service director is a team chief on one of our twelve teams."

"Oh," Congressman Wolk said. "Well, should I ask where all the communications and for that matter vehicles are coming from to support those teams?"

"That was easy. We, ah," and he paused for a second, "we borrowed them from the Navy, Secret Service and FBI."

"You borrowed them?" Frank questioned.

"Yes, Sir, just until this mission is complete and if we need any additional equipment or supplies, they will be provided. You can rest assured that no resources needed to provide protection for General Darwin will be denied to our groups. That I can assure you."

Frank shook his head. "Who will be my go-between for these teams?" he asked.

"I will," the man answered.

"Where do you work?" Congressman Wolk asked.

"I'm on the president's detail," the man replied, "and you can contact me at any time at this number."

Then looking straight at Congressman Wolk he said, "Sir, no one if we can help it will harm General Darwin. Not on our watch." And with that he stood and left the room.

Chapter 20

Norm and Arydin sat in the control tower and listened to the tape again then turned to the controller.

"You said the pilot declared an in-flight emergency. When did he do it and how far out was he from the airport?" Arydin asked.

"Their radar showed him about forty miles west of us and we lost him on radar for a few minutes at about thirty miles out. But as you can see, he made it to the airport nosediving into that hanger. The fire destroyed the aircraft and hanger."

"Have you been able to determine how many people were in that aircraft?" Norm asked.

"Not really," the controller replied. Our fire chief thinks there was only one person onboard but we will have to wait for the fire to cool down to verify that."

Norm turned to Arydin, "Something's not right. If the pilot had been transporting the courier, there should be two bodies in that plane and I bet the fire chief is correct and there is only one."

Arydin pointed to the large map depicting the area around the airport. "They lost that aircraft for a few minutes about thirty miles west of here right after he declared an emergency."

They both turned to the controller and Arydin asked, "Do you know of any private landing strips in that area?"

The man looked at the map, pointed to an area approximately thirty miles east of the airport and answered, "The Gibson family has a dirt airstrip in that area. It's on Route 9 about thirty-two miles from us."

Norm grabbed his cell phone and a moment later had Protelly on the other end. The discussion only lasted seconds and then he hung up.

"Arydin, we have to get to that airfield now. Protelly has his people on the way as we speak."

He turned to the controller, "Notify our pilot," then stopped, "no, we can't use that aircraft. It can't land on that airstrip. Do you have a small aircraft we can have operational in a few minutes?"

"Hell, I have a dozen of them out there waiting for FAA to lift its quarantine. Take your pick."

In minutes, Norm and Arydin were in a Cessna four-passenger aircraft and taxiing out to the runway.

The pilot turned and looked back at them, "I don't know who you guys are but I understand whatever you are up to is very important or the FAA would have never let me off this airport so where are we going?"

Norm pointed to a spot on the map and replied, "There's a small dirt landing strip near a farmhouse in that area. Find it and drop us off. I should warn you this could be dangerous and if you want out now is the time."

The pilot didn't even answer, just turned onto the runway and lifted off. Within a few minutes the plane was circling the dirt landing strip.

"Ok guys, here's your dirt strip. What's next?"

"We need you to land and taxi near the hangar and drop us off. Don't stop completely and as soon as we're on the ground get the hell out of there."

The pilot said, "Look guys, I spent twenty years in the Air Force and if there is anything else I can do, all you have to do is ask."

Norm put his hand on the pilot's shoulder, "Thanks but you have done enough. Just put us on the ground."

"Roger that," the pilot replied and as he started his descent, he saw both of his passengers draw pistols and click off the safeties. Well, he thought, someone is going to catch hell.

He landed next to an open hanger and turned his aircraft around. By the time he opened the throttle and started back down the runway his passengers were gone.

Norm and Arydin hung close to the outer wall of the hangar, away from the farmhouse, and watched until the aircraft lifted into the sky. Then it became strangely quiet.

"Well, Norm," Arydin asked, "what do we do now?" And Norm pointed to the farmhouse.

****

The attempt on Lieutenant General Wendy Darwin's life took place in the Senate Capitol Building. She had just left her car in the garage and was in the elevator with several other people. As the elevator doors opened three men

84

stepped out of a doorway approximately one hundred yards away and pulled weapons from their coats, opening fire at the elevator door.

Before Wendy could react, she was slammed to the floor and rolled to the inside wall of the elevator with a body covering her.

She could hear gunfire both inside and outside the elevator and from the corner of her eye saw several people slump to the floor just as they ran from the elevator. As she tried to raise, she heard a female voice above her.

"Don't move, General Darwin. We have you in the safest place in the elevator. Stay put until I tell you otherwise."

She heard the confidence in the woman's voice and edged as close to the wall as she could. As she turned her head, she could not see the woman above her but two men lay flat on the floor firing their weapons out the door. Moments later the elevator doors closed and the elevator slowly started to descend. The exchange of gunfire seemed to have gone on for a long time but she knew from her training that it had lasted for only a few seconds.

She heard the woman's voice say, "You can get up, General Darwin, but I want you to stay behind me until we are out of this elevator." She then turned to one of the men who had risen with a gun in his hand and moved toward her. Wendy heard her ask what about Tim and the man shook his head. Wendy then saw the blood seeping around the head of the man lying on the floor.

When the elevator stopped the woman spoke into a microphone on her collar and Wendy had her first look at the female. She was about five-foot five-inches tall, one hundred twenty pounds, red hair and an air of supreme confidence surrounding her.

Just before the doors opened, she turned and Wendy could see the slate-grey eyes which seemed to look right through her.

Wendy saw the concern in her eyes as she asked, "Have you been injured, Ma'am?"

"No," Wendy replied.

Outside the door stood six men and women all with guns in their hands and four had their backs to her as if on lookout.

One of the men stated, "The area upstairs has been contained and neutralized but we need to get General Darwin out of the building."

"Hold on," Wendy stated. "I am not going anywhere but to my office. Before I do I want some answers." And no one could miss the authority in her voice.

The young woman turned to her, "Ma'am, I'm Tonya Becker, special agent with the FBI. I and this team, and she pointed to those around her, are one of several that have been covertly assigned to provide protection for you."

"Who authorized that Wendy ask?"

"Well," Tonya replied with a smile, "I am not sure authorized is the right word. Let's just say it was requested by Congressman Wolk."

"Well, I would like to say I don't need protection but after what just happened up there, I know better. The problem is I was going to setup some type of security but I did not think they would strike this fast. I knew I could be a target, thanks to the president telling the world I had been in-charge of tracking down the terrorist.

"Who's in charge of this detail?"

"I am," Tonya replied.

"Is your agent in the elevator dead?" Wendy asks.

"I'm afraid so, Ma'am."

"I want his name and that of his family if he has one."

"Yes, Ma'am," Tonya replied.

"Was any other of your other agents hurt?"

Tonya hesitated for a second, "Only me, Ma'am, and it's only a scratch."

Wendy looked at Tonya Becker and saw the blood dripping from her left hand. She walked over and pulled the left sleeve of her coat off and saw where the bullet had grazed her arm just above the elbow.

"You need to have your medical people look at that as soon as possible," Wendy ordered.

"Yes, Ma'am," Tonya replied, "just as soon as my shift is over and not a minute before. This is my team and we will all stay until relieved."

Wendy knew by the tone of the woman's voice that she nor her team were going anyplace.

She sighed, "Very well, Tonya, have your team blend into the background but you come with me to my office."

When they arrived in her office, Congressman Wolk was waiting for them. "Are you all right, Wendy?" he asked.

"Yes, but what about the rest of the people in the elevator?"

"It's not good, Wendy, but if not for those agents it would have been a lot worse. We have two aides' dead and four injured, one seriously. All three of the gunmen are dead as well."

"Any idea who they were?"

"No," Frank replied. "They had no identification on them but they were all white males in their thirties or forties. The FBI is running their fingerprints so we may have some news in an hour or two."

"All right, Frank, will you send one of the house medical staff up here with a needle and some thread? This young lady needs her arm sewed up."

"Of course," Frank replied and as he turned to leave, she stopped him.

"And, Frank, thank you. You saved my life."

And he smiled and left the room.

A few minutes later she heard a knock on her door and watched as a young man entered. He asked where the patient was.

Wendy pointed to Tonya and within minutes he had taken care of the wound and Tonya left.

The doctor turned to Wendy, "Ma'am, my name is Dr. Schwentker and I have been assigned by congress to be your private physician. From here on wherever you go, I am to be with you." And he left her without any other explanation.

Chapter 21

Norm and Arydin moved slowly toward a corner of the farmhouse, in an attempt to stay out of sight of the windows so as not to give anyone inside a clear shot at them. As Norm started forward to look in the window Arydin suddenly grabbed him.

He whispered, "The place is wired." And he pointed to a small thin wire leading from the window sill to the ground.

"Christ!" Norm said and moved back a few steps.

"Now what?" Arydin asked.

Norm heard sounds of helicopters overhead and within seconds several helicopters were landing around the farmhouse.

Norm reached for his cell phone, punched in the number and watched as armed FBI agents hit the ground, weapons pointed at the farmhouse and at Norm and Arydin. Both men just stood there with their arms raised above their heads.

A few seconds later they saw Agent Protelly move toward them and they could see he was madder than hell.

His first words were, "Are you two trying to get killed?" Then, "Shit, if you had not called me my people could have shot you before they knew who you were. What the hell were you thinking?"

"Well," Arydin replied with a slight grin, "it was Norm's idea. He figured we might be able to surround the house until help arrived," and before Protelly could explode he continued, "by the way you need to tell your people that house is rigged with explosives."

It took an hour for the EOD team to deactivate the explosives and, after searching the house, all that was found were the bodies of the couple who owned the farm. Both had been shot execution style with a bullet to the head and their bodies dumped in the basement. During that time, Protelly had his people canvassing the neighborhood trying to pick up any leads.

****

The three of them now sat in the FBI's mobile command post van watching as they posted information on a large screen.

Norm finally commented, "From what we see here it looks like our man has managed to escape again and each time with help and that is really starting to bother me. We started this hunt with only a couple of people involved yet, each time we get close more people are popping out of the woodwork. That tells me the cell that is supporting him grows larger each day. They are well-coordinated, professional and efficient in moving the courier along, but to where?

Protelly spoke up at that point, "From what my people have found out, that plane landed on this strip for just a few seconds, so one of the neighbors said and then continued on to the airport. That means the courier probably got off here. Another neighbor stated she saw a light tan van leave this farmhouse a few minutes later heading west and the only large city west of here is Burlington, Iowa. I have my people searching for the van but now it looks like it vanished."

Arydin said, "As smart as these people are, they probably ditched that van not too far from here and continued their journey in another vehicle."

"I think you are probably right," Protelly stated, "and I have my people looking in every barn and garage they can find within twenty-five miles of here. But nothing has been found so far."

"The man has at least a three-hour head start on us," Norm replied. "And it looks like we've lost his trail. We had better pick it back up fast." With that he stood and walked out the door.

A few minutes later, Arydin followed and as he left the mobile command post he saw Norm leaning against the car with that faraway look in his eyes. When he approached, Norm turned and looked at him.

"Arydin, something's not right. I can feel it but I can't put my finger on it. We're missing part of the puzzle but what?"

Arydin just shook his head.

****

The driver drove the light tan van up close to the edge of the Mississippi River in a desolate area used mostly by local fishermen. As the courier left the vehicle, the driver put the van in gear and the two men watched as the vehicle plunged into the river and disappeared.

COLD WIND

A few minutes later a high-powered speedboat slowly moved toward them and seconds later both men were in the boat heading down river toward St. Louis, Missouri.

Chapter 22

Ed Manson stood by the door of the Oval Office saying nothing as President Baker continued his tirade.

"It's not my fault someone tried to assassinate General Darwin so why are the American people blaming me? Have you seen the papers?" And he picked up several and threw them back down on the desk. "The news stations are crucifying me." With a whine to his voice he continued, "It's not my fault. Why can't they see that?"

Ed thought, if you had not fired her this probably would not have happened, but he kept the thought to himself.

"Ed, we have to do something to show the White House, and more important the president, is enraged over this incident."

Again, Ed thought, I don't think trying to assassinate General Darwin is an incident, but he said nothing.

"Ed, set up a meeting with the press. I want to go on national TV by noon and talk with the American people."

"Do you want me to write the speech for you, Sir?"

"No," the president replied, "I will do it myself."

Oh boy, Ed thought as he left the room. I hope he does better than the last time he tried that.

****

As Norm and Arydin drove back to the airport, Norm looked at his friend and then shook his head. "We are missing something, Arydin. I can feel it but I cannot figure out what it is. I have been going over everything that has happened in the past six days since we started tracking this guy and the only thing that keeps popping in my head is a nagging feeling that they are leading us down a primrose path. This is a path we should not be on. Does that make any sense?"

Arydin smiled, "Norm, I always said you have the instincts of a bloodhound when you set your sights on something. And I tend to agree with you because every time we get close to this guy, he drops into a hole only to

93

surface someplace else. It reminds me of a bird who is sitting on her nest with a clutch of young. A fox comes by and the bird lures it away from the nest by pretending to have a broken wing. The Fox goes for the bird thinking it's an easy meal and the diversion almost always works."

"Damn! I think that's it, Arydin," Norm shouted. "The bastard is luring us away but from where?"

Before Arydin could answer, Norm's cell phone sounded. When he slowly lowered it, he told Arydin about the attack on Wendy.

"She wants us to return to Washington as soon as possible."

****

When they arrived at Andrews Air Force Base, they were surprised at what they saw. As they left the aircraft, at the bottom of the staircase was a nondescript vehicle with two men in casual clothes waiting for them.

They motioned them into the car and within minutes they were on the beltway heading toward Washington. The individual in the passenger seat turned toward them and introduced himself as Joe and stated he and the driver, who he did not name, were taking them to see Ms. Darwin. And with that he turned back to look out the front window. Norm and Arydin noticed he was keeping a watch out the side rearview mirror as well.

No other discussion occurred until thirty minutes into the drive, Norm suddenly asked, "Where are you taking us? You just passed the turnoff to Washington."

Upon entering the vehicle at the airport Norm had taken his pistol from its holster and placed it on the right side of his leg where his hand now laid on its handle grip. Arydin had done the same. Acting slowly and deliberately, Norm did not think either man had noticed.

Without turning around the man in the front passenger seat replied to Norm's question. "General Darwin has been moved outside of the city for her own safety and that's where we're going now. The safehouse is about thirty minutes farther." And with that the driver turned off the beltway onto I-66 west.

"By the way," the man stated, "you two can put your weapons away. They will not be needed," and he chuckled as he continued to look out the side mirror.

Arydin had also been watching their back through the front rearview mirror since they had left the airport and now said, "I have a question. I noticed the red car about five cars back who picked us up after we left the airport but what about the blue van about seven cars behind him? He also has not left us as we turned onto the beltway."

"Shit!" the man said as he turned and looked out the back window. Then said, "Keep your weapons handy." Then he spoke into a microphone located on his shirt collar.

Some ten minutes later as they passed an exit from the interstate, Norm watched as several cars blended in with the traffic. He also noticed that most of the vehicles either kept pace or passed their car but four cars were slowly allowing the traffic to pass them.

Arydin turned to Norm and said, "It looks like they have the van blocked in."

And then all hell broke loose. Neither man could hear sounds but both could suddenly see the gun flashes erupting from the blue Van and the return fire from the vehicles. The blue van suddenly careened off the interstate and rolled over several times in the medium. They also saw several vehicles follow the van into the medium, and then they lost this view as their vehicle turned off the interstate onto a secondary road.

Norm heard the man in the front seat say to the driver, "The threat has been neutralized but the bastards were good, almost too good. If it had not been for our friends back there, I'm not sure we would have spotted them."

He turned and looked at Arydin for a long moment, then smiled and said, "We owe you."

Norm and Arydin had the feeling they had just been granted entry into a very special club and, in a way, they had.

Some twenty minutes later, they turned off the secondary road onto a dirt lane. Soon they crossed a one-lane bridge then entered a small forest of trees. From the secondary road it appeared as if they had just disappeared for no trace of their vehicle could be seen.

Arydin and Norm were surprised when the vehicle slowed to a stop near a small clearing. Their companions gave them an order to leave the car, and even more alarmed when the vehicle slowly turned around and left the way it had come, just leaving them standing by themselves.

Norm turned and looked at Arydin then said, "I don't like this."

"Neither do I," Arydin replied and both men drew guns and started edging for the line of trees a few feet away.

Chapter 23

Congressman Wolk had just left the House chambers when a page intercepted him. He read the note, thanked the page and returned to the chambers. Within minutes he had several of his colleagues in tow guiding them to one of the conference rooms located just outside the chamber.

The men and women situated around the room were all colleagues from both parties but more important they were close friends, some for twenty years or more.

He pulled the note from his pocket and commence to tell them of the attempt on Lieutenant Shepherd and Arydin's lives on the Dulles Toll Road and the five men who had attempted it. It appears they were all from the Middle East and for the past two years had lived in Lansing Michigan.

"What some of you may know is that's the same community the man we have been tracking for the past several days also came from," Congressman Wolk said.

"Once those men left Lansing, Michigan yesterday they were under constant surveillance by the FBI. Last night they checked into the Amber Mattel here in Washington and early this morning disappeared. From what the FBI has been able to determine they individually changed their appearance and left the hotel from different locations and different times. They left their vehicle in the hotel garage.

"When they were spotted on the Dulles Toll Road this morning they were driving in a blue Van. So, they had some help last night and the FBI is now attempting to find out where that help came from.

"When our people intercepted them, a gunfight ensued and when it was over all five of them were dead."

One of the women in the group spoke up, "So where does that leave us now?"

Congressman Wolk looked around the room and stated, "We are in a major crisis, the country is in turmoil and we are leaderless as far as the president is concerned. He's sitting there in the White House hoping all this will just go way. Well, it's not going away and it's time Congress stood up to defend our country because the president will not.

"All of you here have control over major committees that help guide this country and now is the time we accept that authority. First, we need the Supreme Court to act on the president's order to deport all the Muslims in this country and more importantly at this point to stop him from placing them in detention centers. Either way the court must act now, today if possible.

"Second, before we have a major rebellion on our hands from the American people toward the Muslims living in this country, we need to come up with a plan to protect all of our citizens."

****

It startled them when they heard the voice behind them say, "You can put your weapons away. You are in no danger."

Both men turned and saw the young woman standing there. Norm's first thought was how did she manage to come up behind them without them knowing she was there.

Arydin on the other hand was staring at the most beautiful woman he had ever seen. She was small in stature, petite around five feet tall but you could not miss that she was a full-grown woman but that was not what Arydin was staring at. Her features were of Middle Eastern heritage. Her eyes appeared to be almost coal black, her skin tone was like a dusky brown tone and her black hair flowed around her face like a halo.

Her eyes locked with his, the whole time since he had turned. Suddenly Arydin felt the heat creep across his face as an ever so slight smile began to form on her lips.

Norm stood watching the two of them and finally muttered as if to remind them he was there. "OK, now what?"

The woman turned and looked at him. "Norm, it's nice to meet you."

Then she turned and looked again at Arydin, "It's a pleasure to meet you, Arydin. I have heard a lot about you."

With that she turned and walked into the woods as she said, "Please follow me. Stay close and do not wander from the trail."

Some fifteen minutes later, the three of them stood facing a large granite rock set in the hillside. They watched in amazement as the young woman touched the bolder and a panel slid aside exposing a small opening. She again turned to them, "From this point on you will receive your instructions from inside the facility. Please go through the entrance now."

Norm looked at Arydin then the woman and with a wary look pointed at the entrance as he reached for his gun, "Arydin, you go first and I'll follow."

The woman stepped forward and raised her hand, "Mr. Shepard, please do not do that. You would be dead before it cleared your holster."

"What the hell!" Arydin shouted. "We're not taking another step until we have some answers. What is this place, why are we here and who are you?"

It appeared at first that she would answer then she raised her left hand to her ear as if listening to something. She finally turned and walked into the opening in the rock leaving them standing there.

"Christ, now what?" Norm exclaimed.

"I don't know but I sure don't like it," Arydin stated. "We have two choices, either follow her or get the hell out of here. And I am beginning to think the latter is the smartest option."

I agree with you but hell, Arydin, whoever they are, I don't think they intend to harm us. If they intended to do that, they could have done it before now."

"Ok, so where do we go from here?"

Norm pointed to the entrance and a few minutes later, both men were in a long tunnel. The entrance had closed as soon as they entered. The walls were smooth and painted white and the ceiling was about eight feet high with a row of lights hanging from it. At the far end of the tunnel, they could see a door recessed into the wall but no sound of any kind, just silence.

Norm looked at Arydin, "You take the left side and I'll take the right. Stay close to the wall." And both men started walking toward the door.

"Well, we made it this far. Now what?" Norm whispered.

"Hell, Norm, it looks like a blast door of some kind and there is no way we're going to break it down." The door appeared to be steel. "It doesn't even have a door knob or handle on it so what do we do now?"

As if to answer, the door slid open and both men snapped to attention. General Wendy Darwin stood on the other side looking at them for a moment and then motioned for them to follow her.

A short time later, they entered a room that contained a small conference table with twelve chairs, several TV screens mounted on the walls and a large digital clock. In one corner was a table that held a large coffee pot and cups. General Darwin motioned for them to take a seat and she left the room.

Minutes later eight people walked in, one being the young woman who had brought them here and FBI Agent Nick Protelly who had a very uncomfortable look on his face. General Darwin asked everyone to take a seat and the young woman took a chair directly across from Arydin and Norm.

Two of the individuals moved to the corner of the room, one on each side of General Darwin and remained standing. One was a man and the other was a woman and Norm thought to himself, now there are two people I would not want to tangle with. Arydin was looking at the woman across from him and again saw the start of a smile before she turned and looked at General Darwin.

"OK people, let's get with it," and she turned to Norm and Arydin. "You both know Agent Protelly and there is only one other person here you need to know and we will get to that in a minute. First, for your information we are currently located in an underground Central Intelligence Agency (CIA) bunker just outside of Washington. It's probably as secure as any of these types of facilities in the country and from now on it's going to be my command post until this crisis is over. Norm, your mother is here as well. I was not going to risk her life if they get close to me again. You can see her when this meeting is over."

Norm just nodded his head.

"Arydin, your mother has a security detail with her as well. She just doesn't know it.

"Now, let me introduce you to Alia Farah. She is an analyst and a covert operation agent for the CIA. She's twenty-four years old and was born in Pakistan. Don't let her age fool you. She has been on several classified operations and four men found out how tough she is. They are not around anymore.

"Norm, at the start of this operation, I asked Alia to follow you two in order to analyze what is going on and try to find out how much of a threat these terrorists are. And I can assure you she probably knows each of you better than you know yourselves. She is that good at her job. She has also come up with some new evidence that we need to address and I will have her brief you in a few minutes.

"Second, it appears I am still a general in the U.S. Air Force. It seems the joint chief of staff has refused to accept my resignation and has told the president that if he wants to remove me from office, he's going to have to do it himself. That is something he has refused to do, up until now, anyway. Not sure how that is all going to come out. We'll just have to wait and see.

"Now, Alia, would you please brief us on what you have found out and more important what you think these terrorists are attempting to do."

Alia did not move from her chair and it seemed as if she was talking to an invisible person in the room. Her voice had a soft quality to it when she said, "Please dim the lights and lower the screen."

The room went dark and a large screen silently slid down the wall in front of her. There on the screen were pictures of Norm, Arydin and Nick Protelly and a complete bio of each under their picture.

Norm thought, damn she's good. There's information up there that I don't think my mom knows.

Arydin puzzled as to how she obtained the information, some of which even he had forgotten long ago.

Protelly on the other hand, was not pleased with what he saw. If the lights were brighter, everyone could have seen the flush on his face.

Before anyone could comment on the information they were seeing, Alia stated, "Based on this information we have in our database, I do not think General Darwin could have picked a better team for the task at hand. It appears that we have these terrorist on the run and if you believe that you would be wrong."

"What?" Protelly blurted out. "What do you base that on? We are close to apprehending the courier and when we do, we will be able to close this case."

Before he could continue, General Darwin stated, "Agent Protelly, let her finish." And with that Agent Protelly promptly sat back down.

Alia continued, "I would agree with you, Agent Protelly, except for one thing. I do not believe that the courier is the main threat. In fact, I believe he is a decoy and the main threat is elsewhere."

Norm spoke up, "I think she may be right. I have had this feeling for the past couple of days that we're missing something but can't figure out what. Do you know what we're missing, Alia?"

"I think I do, Norm. Let me explain." With that a new picture flashed on the screen, a map of the United States. You will all notice that I have outlined the trail the courier has used up until this point and the others who crashed their plane in Montana. Do any of you see a pattern here?"

Arydin spoke up, "I believe I do. It's not the trail we are looking at but the ease in which we have been following it. Christ, looking back it's as if he has purposely stayed just one step ahead of us. But why?"

"I think I can answer that, Arydin," Alia replied.

She turned to Agent Protelly, "Can you give me a ballpark figure on how many agents you have working this case?"

"Yes," Protelly replied, "close to twenty thousand agents."

"How many agents do you have in the Bureau?"

"Twenty-five thousand," he replied.

"So, now most of your agents are located close to the eastern part of the country."

"Yes," Protelly answered as he began to get a sinking feeling in his stomach.

"So," Norm said, "If the courier is purposely drawing our resources toward the East Coast, what is his rational for doing so? He knows he cannot continue to keep it up and sooner or later, we are going to catch him.

"Damn," he continued almost as if to himself, "his target is not the East Coast, or even if it is, it's only a decoy." He looked at the map and pointed. "The real target must be the West Coast. It's heavily populated but thinly protected and that's my fault. I directed all those assets to follow the courier."

Norm was now feeling like an idiot and did not know what to say. He turned to General Darwin, "General, I screwed this up pretty badly and request you relieve me of any further duties regarding this assignment. Hell, Alia has figured out what we now think the terrorists are up to and she hasn't even been involved in what has been going on."

Arydin stood, "General, I agree with Norm and feel I should be relieved as well."

General Darwin observed the two men for a moment and then said, "Lieutenant Shepard, Lieutenant Hassan, I assigned both of you the task of finding these terrorists and neither of you are going anywhere until you finish that task. Is that clear?"

"Yes, Ma'am," both men replied.

"Now, Lieutenant Shepard, you are correct that Alia has not been actively on the ground following you two but there was a reason for that. I wanted someone on the outside looking in to independently see what was going on. While you two had your nose to the ground, so to speak, she was looking at the overall picture. That's what analysts do and as I said earlier, she is the best the CIA has. I would have been disappointed if she had not found what she did and as far as not being on the ground, I'm going to rectify that right now. Ali is assigned to your team as we speak. She will take her orders from either you, Lieutenant Shepard or Lieutenant Hassan and no one else, neither her agency or any other agency or the Department of Defense. Is that understood?"

"Yes, Ma'am," both men again replied.

"Very well. Now, Alia, give us the bad news, based on your analysis."

"Yes, Ma'am," and she turned back to the screen. "If you will look at the crash site in Montana, I believe that aircraft was not heading directly for the West Coast but more probably the North-West Coast, either Oregon or Washington State. My rationale for this is because of what I found in California. Your people found where the Anthrax came from but then turned your attention to tracking where that substance was going. I know, Agent Protelly, that your people found the source for bringing that agent into the country and the work your people did in attempting to find if anyone else was involved in the plot, including searching that crew members sleeping quarters."

Then she dropped the bombshell. "There was something that I just could not put my finger on so I had some of our people take a closer look at that ship and I found that under layers of ownership, that ship is owned by one of the major terrorist organizations in the Middle East.

"To make matters worse, that ship left the West Coast two days ago and yesterday it declared an emergency about twenty miles off the coast of California. The captain radioed our Coast Guard that they are waiting for a part to fix their engine and it should arrive within one or two days.

They are just outside our twelve-mile limit, in international waters, and that ship is setting just outside of Los Angles. What's important about this is the wind direction. If you wanted to disperse a biological agent and you wanted to use that method, where do you disperse the agent to start with? The wind flows from the West Coast to the East Coast. If that ship is the carrier for the agent, they could release the agent and before it was over they could contaminate the whole West Coast and I don't know how far inland."

Stunned silence filled the room.

"If that's the case then I need to start moving a large- number of my people to the West Coast as soon as possible," Agent Protelly stated.

"No," General Darwin replied. "You are to continue your task of finding and capturing the courier and it must be done within the next twenty-four to thirty-six hours. And when you do find him, I want the American people informed that he was killed in a gun battle with your agents. That's for public consumption. What I really want if possible is for your people to capture him alive and let the other terrorists think he's dead. It may buy us a little more time," and in a flat cold voice stated, "I would like to have a little talk with that individual."

"But," Protelly replied, "I still need to start moving our agents to the West Coast as soon as possible."

"If you did that," General Darwin replied, "you would probably tip off the terrorist to the fact that we know where the real threat is coming from. I know we need more resources on the West Coast but I want it done covertly. So, come up with a plan where we can start moving them into place discreetly. And I will say it again, I don't want the terrorist to know they are coming and I don't want them to know the FBI is there in force."

"Yes, Ma'am," Protelly answered but everyone could tell he was not happy about it.

General Darwin then turned to Norm and Arydin, "If Alia is right, and I believe she is, then we need to find out everything we can about that ship and if possible, when and how they intend to attack this country. Do you have any problems with that order?"

"No, Ma'am," both men replied.

"Very well. Then I have a helicopter standing by a few miles from here to take the three of you and Agent Protelly if he wants to go to Charlottesville. There an unmarked aircraft is standing by to take you to Los Angles."

Protelly spoke up, "General, if it is all the same to you, I wish to go with them but I have two questions. First, am I still a part of this assignment?"

"Yes," General Darwin replied and I would have been surprised if you did not go. You still have full control of all your agents and the working relationship you have with Norm and Arydin continues as it has in the past."

"Very well, Ma'am, and how does the president fit into all this?"

"I will take care of the president." she said and left the room.

Chapter 24

President Baker was literally screaming at his Chief of Staff, Ed Manson. "Who the hell does she think she is? I am the president of the United States and no one is going to tell me what I can or cannot do."

Ed had finally reached the boiling point and shouted at the president, "Well, Sir, if you still wish to remain president you had damn well better listen to her. She has effectively turned the congress against you and that includes the members of your own party. She has convinced congress to put a hold on your deportation plan which the majority agrees with and she has the full backing of all our military armed forces. Hell, if she wanted, she could request impeachment proceedings against you. And if she did, you would be out of office within twenty-four hours.

"I'm surprised she has not already done it. So, Mr. President, I would highly recommend you meet with her as she requested. Your presidency may very well depend on it. My letter of resignation will be on your desk within the hour." and he turned and left the room. leaving the president sitting in stunned silence.

Some two hours later the president and Ed Manson entered the Presidential Emergency Operations Center (PEOC) where General Darwin sat at the conference table. She did not rise as they entered. For a long moment she stared at both men and then signed and motioned for them to sit. The president started to head for the chair at the head of the table which had the presidential seal on it but General Darwin stopped him and pointed to the chair across from her. The president's face turned red with the flush that crossed it and he hesitated a moment before he turned and went to the chair she indicated.

Ed kept the smile off his face but knew she had just let the president know who was in charge here and it was not the president. He had been surprised when the president had not accepted his letter of resignation and more so when he had pleaded with him to stay on. He did not take a chair but rather took a stance in the far corner of the room and waited.

When General Darwin spoke, her voice was soft but you could feel the steel in the words, "Mr. President, what I have to say is only between you and me," and she glanced at Ed as if to say forget anything you hear or get out.

Ed smiled and folded his arms and leaned against the wall. She only nodded and turned back to the president.

"Mr. President, this country is in mortal danger of being attacked within the next forty-eight hours and if the terrorists succeed millions of our citizens will die."

President Baker started to say something and she stopped him.

"Let me finish and I will answer any questions you have if I can.

"During this crisis we need strong and effective leadership at the highest levels of our government which includes your office leading the way but because of your stubbornness and ego, we do not have the leadership we need to fight this danger to our country."

The president's face turned a bright red but he said nothing as she continued.

"At this very moment congress is preparing impeachment proceedings and if it should continue, you will no longer be in office by this time tomorrow. Is that what you want?"

The president slowly rose from his chair and in a trembling voice said, "No, that is not what I want. But I do not know what to do to stop what is going on in the country," and he slumped back down in his chair.

Wendy looked at the man for a long moment and then stated, "I will attempt to stop the impeachment procedures but in return there are several things you must do. First, stop this nonsense of deporting the Muslims living in our country. Second, I understand you intend to go back on National TV today. Fine, do so, but I will write the speech for you to give to the nation. Third, put your national security council in charge of this crises and approve all recommendations they send to you. Finally, you will agree to not run for a second term as president of these United States. The choice is yours," and she stood waiting for his answer.

All the president said was, "I agree."

And General Wendy Darwin walked out of the room.

****

Norm, Protelly, Arydin and Alia sat around the table watching the president on TV as he outlined his plan for stopping the terrorist from attacking the country.

After the press conference, Norm looked at the group. "Well, Arydin and you too Alia, it looks like you're off the hook for being deported. I wonder what changed his mind?"

Alia smiled, "I think you know the answer to that question."

"Yes, I think I do," he replied. "In any event let's hope the last part of his speech has convinced the terrorist we have taken the bait."

"I hope so," Nick stated. "If they believe we are using most of our resources to find the courier here on the East Coast they will not be on the lookout for many of us on the West Coast."

"Alia, your thoughts?" Norm asked.

"I think you're right, Nick. If they believe most of our people are looking for them on the East Coast, we may catch them off guard and hopefully stop the main attack before they can complete it."

"Well," Arydin replied. It still does not solve the problem of the courier who still has enough Anthrax to kill one hell of a lot of our people."

Protelly spoke, "I think he finally made a mistake. Just before we came into this meeting, I received a call from one of my agents and he said our command post had received a call from a local fisherman who stated he was fishing on the Mississippi River a couple of hours ago and saw two men across the river push a car into the water. A few minutes later, he saw a high-speed motor boat pull up and the two men climbed onto the boat and it took off down river. That incident occurred about twenty miles from the farm where we lost the courier."

Norm shook his head. "But we really don't know if that was the courier. It could just as easily have been a crime of some other type."

Alia said, "Based on the calculations I came up with on the computer, it states it's a 92 percent chance that it was the courier who got in that boat. Also based on my calculations, if the boat with help from the river current can maintain a speed of approximately sixty miles per hour they could reach St. Louis, Missouri in about three hours." The men just looked at her for a moment.

Then Protelly said, "Norm, if St. Louis is the target we have very little time in which to intercept him. Or it could be just another way-stop to his destination, wherever the hell that may be."

Norm walked to the large map of the area. "OK, Alia, can you get two drones from your assets to cover that river from here to St. Louis?"

"Done," she replied.

"Will those drones be armed?"

"Yes," she replied.

"Protelly, can you move as many of your people as you can to cover both banks of the river for thirty miles upriver from St. Louis?"

"I started that twenty minutes ago," he responded.

"Very good people, let's see if we can finally catch this guy or kill him," Norm commented.

"I need to brief General Darwin so, Arydin, we need some type of plan on what action we're going to take to neutralize the threat on the West Coast." Norm had added.

Arydin just waved his hand and Norm left the room.

****

The courier sat in the boat feeling it race down the river for the past two hours. He suddenly turned to his companion. "I don't like this. We are too exposed. Is there a backup to using the boat?"

"Yes," the man replied. About every twenty miles or so, we have personnel on the river bank ready to pick you up if the need should arise. They are disguised as fishermen if anyone should see them."

"Where is the closest one to where we are now?" he asked.

"Near the town of Cape Girardeau, about ten miles from here," he replied.

"Go there," the courier ordered.

****

General Darwin suddenly returned to the CIA conference room and directed Norm's group to watch the large TV. As they sat there, they suddenly saw a large river and then a boat racing on it. Suddenly the boat exploded in a ball of fire. Then the TV went blank.

"Now, tell me what you saw?" she questioned.

Nick Protelly was the first to say, "Well, if that was the boat the courier was in, we finally got him. There is no way he could have survived that explosion. The Anthrax was either destroyed in the fireball or in the water where it would have been neutralized."

Norm had an odd feeling and he saw the puzzled look on Arydin's face but before either man could say anything, Alia rose.

"I think we may have lost him again," she stated.

"What is your rational for that?" General Darwin asked.

"If you look closely at the boat the only person in it appears to be the driver. Two men besides the driver got in that boat so where are the other two? Also, when they started out, they were heading down river yet if you look closely at the film, you can see the boat was heading up river when it was destroyed. To me, that means the courier got off at some point and I think it was not too long before the boat was destroyed. If we have satellite imagery on the river, it should tell us when and where that occurred."

Damn, Norm thought, she is good. I saw the boat was empty but missed the boat going back up river.

The general nodded, "I think you're right, Alia, and as of now I will take over finding the courier. I want the four of you to concentrate on eliminating the threat on the West Coast. And Mr. Protelly, I intend to use only a hundred or so of your FBI agents. The rest are yours to use on the West Coast."

"Yes, Ma'am," Protelly said as the general left the room.

Norm could tell Protelly was not a happy man. "Nick, don't take this personal. All the general did was take a portion of the problem off our shoulders so we can more effectively concentrate on the major problem."

"Yea, I know," Nick replied, but I really wanted to catch that bastard."

"I know," Norm replied. "So, did I."

Nearly four hours later, the four-member team was in California.

Chapter 25

General Darwin had been watching the white van on the large screen as it moved east on Highway 152 until it turned north on Highway 51 in Illinois.

She turned to the man standing behind the podium and simply asked, "What is the agency's view on where he's going?"

"General Darwin, we had a drone monitoring the boat that the suspected terrorist was in when it suddenly turned to the Illinois side of the river, about thirty miles south of St. Louis, Missouri. The boat pulled up next to land and two individuals left the boat. They joined three other men in the white van that you have been watching on the screen. The boat then turned and headed back upstream. Approximately ten minutes later, a hellfire missile launched from a drone destroyed the boat," and he hesitated for a second before he stated, "per your instructions."

General Darwin turned to the man, "Are you telling me the van was not being observed while the boat was destroyed?"

"No, Ma'am. We had a second drone in the area as a backup and it is the transmission from this drone you are watching. Based on the direction the van is traveling, and if it does not radically change direction, we believe it's heading for Chicago, Illinois."

"Why?" General Darwin asked.

"Ma'am, if they stay on Highway 51 near the town of Vandalia, they will intersect with I-57 and if they stay on it, it goes directly into Chicago."

"If you are correct, then what are your recommendations for stopping them?"

"Well, Ma'am, our agency cannot by law take personal action against the target because it is on U.S. soil. So, it would have to be the FBI who would have to apprehend them or under the circumstances you may be able to use the military."

"We will let the FBI do it but do you have a plan that we can use to accomplish it? Time is of the essence so do we have to wait for the FBI to come up with one?"

"No, Ma'am. We think there is a way to intercept the van and prevent the occupants from escaping without using excessive force. We had the drone who destroyed the boat start monitoring Highway 51 ahead of that vehicle and found a stretch of road we can use to stop the van. As you can see on the screen, there's an area not far from Vernon, Illinois and about twenty-five miles south of I-57 that is mostly farmland, not heavily populated and in this area here."

She watched the images from the drone's camera as it zoomed onto a bridge, several hundred feet long, that stretched over a small stream.

"There are small access roads at both ends of the bridge. Once the van starts across the bridge, we can block both ends and trap the van. It would have nowhere to go. The creek below the bridge at this time of year has very little water flowing through it, so personnel could be available to take out anyone who attempted to escape that way."

General Darwin stood gazing at the screen for a moment and then remarked, "It's a good plan. Let's do it. If I'm not mistaken, Chicago is about seven hundred miles from Washington DC. Is that not correct?"

"Yes, Ma'am, he replied."

"Do we have one of our new jets, the SR-97 located at Dulles International Airport?'

"The Air Force has two located there on stand-by status until this crisis is over, Ma'am."

Wendy knew the SR-97s' had a top speed of over two thousand miles per hour which would give her more than enough time for what she planned to do and that was to be at that bridge when the terrorists arrived.

****

The van had no sooner started across the bridge when several vehicles blocked both ends. The driver of the van slammed on the brakes and slid to a stop in the center of the bridge.

Four men immediately exited the van from the sides and back and started firing automatic weapons. They were all dead within a few seconds.

General Darwin stood at the edge of the bridge and placed the bullhorn near her lips. "You have ten seconds to come out of the vehicle or we will destroy it."

Seconds later, they watched as a man opened the passenger side door and slowly walked to the front of the vehicle. In one hand he held a small bag and the other was in his jacket pocket.

General Darwin walked a few feet out on the bridge, stared at the man for a few moments and then asked, "Did you really think you could achieve your goal? But more important, why would you even attempt it?"

He slowly replied, "I may have failed in my mission but the infidels will feel my wrath as the sun goes down and then you will know who won. When we Muslims say Allah Barkla (God is great), we know God is on our side and we cannot lose."

His eyes widened when General Darwin replied in Arabic and then he died instantly before he had a chance to detonate the explosive vest he wore.

One of the FBI agents retrieved the bag he was holding and said, "Two of the quart jars are in there and intact. We will have our hazmat team seal it and have it taken to Edgewood. By the way, what the hell did you say to him?"

She smiled, "God is great," and turned and left.

Chapter 26

Norm stood looking out the large bay window on to the Santa Monica Bay. The fourth-floor hotel room, located in the Marina Del Rey complex was just four or five miles south of Santa Monica, California and ten miles from Los Angeles.

He turned and looked at the people sitting at the large conference table then directed his question to the women standing next to the door.

"How secure is this hotel?"

"About as secure as you can get. We own it. Renters are on the first two floors. We've sealed off the third, fourth and fifth floors for our use only, along with the basement. The top floor is where our screen room and command post are located and all the staff are our own people. The stairwells and elevators can be sealed off from the rest of the hotel within seconds and our people are armed at all times."

Norm turned to Alia, "I assume by our people she is talking about the CIA."

Alia smiled, rose and walked to the window before she answered. "Yes," she replied. "I chose this building for two reasons. First, we should not draw attention to a lot of people coming and going from a hotel and second, but most important, the ship we're interested in is right out there in front of us, some twenty or thirty miles from shore. Because of the haze and distance, you can't see it from this location but you can from the command post just above us.

Norm stood staring out the window for a few moments then said, "I like it. It gives us cover and it's close to our target. Arydin, Protelly any questions?"

Both men just shook their heads.

"OK, people, let's go up to the command post and look at our target."

After the CIA briefing in the command post and the satellite pictures of the ship they had returned to his room. Norm could feel the tension in the room. They all sat staring at him as if to say, well what are we going to do now and he was not sure what to say.

The knock on the door startled them. Alia stood and opened the door. The man on the other side handed her an envelope and shut the door. She stared at it for a moment then turned and handed it to Norm. If anyone was unsure of who's in charge of the group, they weren't now.

Norm read the single sheet of paper then laid it down on the table, "Well it looks like General Darwin solved one of our problems."

Agent Protelly spoke up, "Which problem?"

Norm replied, "It seems she caught up with the courier," he hesitated for a second before adding, "and she killed him."

"What!" Protelly yelled. "Why have I not been notified?"

Norm raised his hand saying, "Nick, sit down. I think you know why. The longer we can keep the news of his death from getting out, the better chance we have of catching the rest of them. It was your people who took him down, Protelly, and they retrieved the last two quart jars of Anthrax. It's already on its way to Edgewood Arsenal. Your people did a very professional job of taking that bastard down. You should be proud of them."

"I am," Protelly replied. "I only wish I had been there when it happened."

Norm then said, "I for one am glad you're here. If we are going to take these people down, it is you and your people who are going to help us accomplish it. Now that was the good news. The rest of the note I am not so sure of. General Darwin talked with the courier for a few minutes before they took him out and his last words were, "I may have failed in my mission but the infidels will feel my wrath as the sun goes down"."

"What the hell does that mean?" Protelly asked.

It was Alia who answered, "I think he was unintentional telling us we don't have much time left and if the attack is scheduled for tonight, there's not enough time to stop it. But I do not believe that is the case."

"Why?" Arydin asked.

"Well, first they killed the courier today before the sun went down and I believe his mission was to pull as many of our resources as possible away from the major target, the West Coast, and until that happened, they would not strike. Second, even if Chicago was his target which is the closest major city to where they stopped him, he would not have had the time to set in motion his attack today before the sun went down.

"So, I believe we have at least twenty-four hours before they intend to strike, maybe more if his target was even further east, but I doubt it. I think we have until sunset tomorrow evening. By then, I think our time is up."

Norm stood up and addressed the group, "Alia, I agree with your assumption and so does General Darwin. She also gave us twenty-four hours to complete our mission. So, let's come up with a plan on how we're going to accomplish it. Whatever we come up with had better work because tens of thousands of lives may depend on it."

Chapter 27

General Darwin felt the anxiety flow through her body as she sat in the underground bunker staring at the transcript of the phone call she had just received from Ehson. This call like the last one was short and cloaked in ambiguity but the message was clear if a person could decipher it. And she was sure that she understood most if not all of it. It read, "Wendy, I wanted to follow up and let you know that most, but not all of your family members who accepted your invitation to visit you in the United States have arrived and the rest should arrive in the next forty-eight hours. They should arrive on the East and West Coasts and hope to meet you soon thereafter. I wish I could be there as well but my schedule could not permit it, maybe next time."

Wendy had sent him this reply, "Thank you Ehson, your thoughtfulness is greatly appreciated and I can assure you we will meet later. Go with God."

Wendy now knew that the attack would not take place for the next forty-eight hours at least but Ehson's comment that all her relatives had not yet arrived set off alarm bells. Until now she had felt that with the loss of the courier and the location of the ship on the West Coast, they had an excellent picture of how the attack on the country would take place. Now, she knew better. Somehow, they had missed an important part of the attack plan or the implementation had not happened yet. Either way, she had better find the answers and find them soon and she reached for the phone.

Chapter 28

Two-hours had passed since Wendy's cryptic message and she requested a call with Norm and his staff. A classified video tele-conference was established between the CIA bunker and the command post in the hotel where Norm and his staff were located.

General Darwin looked at Norm, Arydin, Nick and Alia on the large screen in the conference room from the CIA bunker. They in turn could see her sitting in the bunker.

General Darwin was the first to speak, "Norm, have you and your people come up with a plan to neutralize that ship yet?" she asked.

"I believe we have," he replied.

"Very well, let's hear it."

"Yes, Ma'am." and he turned to Alia, who brought the picture up on the screen. The first thing General Darwin saw was a lone ship that almost seemed deserted, sitting alone in the ocean.

Then Alia stated, "General, as you can see from the drone image which has been monitoring the ship for the past several hours there is little or no activity on the deck of the ship. Periodically, an individual will come into sight on deck but his sole purpose appears to be checking the water line of the ship. He or she never goes near the tarps spread across the deck. What's under those tarps is anyone's guess but we assume it is the system they plan on using to disperse the Anthrax once the attack starts. We also think the individual who shows up on deck is checking to see if anything is in the water close to the ship. Just a guess but it makes sense.

"At present they are approximately twenty-eight miles from the coast and the current is slowly moving them closer to shore. We estimate that twelve hours from now they will be about fourteen miles from the coast, still outside the twelve-mile limit."

Then Norm stated, "But we do not intend to let them get that close. Twelve hours from now that ship, if it's whom we think, will be resting on the bottom of the ocean or what's left of it."

"How?" General Darwin asked.

"After dark tonight, we intend to have Navy Seal Team 7 which is located here on the West Coast plant mines on the hull of the ship and then blow her out of the water. As a backup, we have a Navy submarine now located a thousand yards from her and if the mines do not take it out, the sub will."

"What if that ship is not our target and is in fact what it says it is, a ship with a problem in its engine room?" The general asked. "As unlikely as that seems, based on the information we now have, are we 100 percent sure that ship is our target?"

"We took that into consideration in planning this operation," Norm replied, "and we all agreed that we had to make sure that ship was the threat we think it is."

"But how are you going to make sure it is?" she again asked.

Norm hesitated for just a second before he replied, "When the Navy Seals start placing the explosives to the hull, we're going to have our personnel check and see what's under those tarps tied down on the deck. If we're lucky and not discovered, it should give us the information we need to determine whether or not that ship is the threat."

"Very well, Norm. It sounds like a good plan and I like the backup plan as well. Now have you briefed the Navy Seals what they should or might be looking for under those tarps?"

Again, Norm was silent for a moment before he replied, "No, Ma'am. We have not briefed the Navy Seals on that portion of the mission. The seals will have their hands full placing those mines and whoever checks those tarps needs to know what they are looking for."

"OK, who has been assigned the task of accomplishing that?" she asked.

Norm replied, "In order to insure we obtain the information we're seeking, I decided that Arydin and I will be the ones who check those tarps. We both have received that type of training at the Academy and we know or will know if what is under those tarps is part of the plan to attack the United States."

Norm was not sure how General Darwin was going to react to that information as he waited for her response.

"Is that the consensus of your group, Norm?"

Before Norm could answer, Nick Protelly said, "I don't like it. Too many things could go wrong and we could lose one or both."

General Darwin was silent for a moment then asked, "Alia, and what are your thoughts on the subject?"

"Ma'am, I have run the scenario through the computer and there appears to be a 78 percent success rate on accomplishing the task but I also would prefer they send someone else to check out those tarps."

Finally, she asked Arydin for his input on the subject.

"Ma'am," he replied, "as Norm stated, both of us are qualified in underwater training. Both of us know what type of equipment we 're looking for and anything that could be used to deploy Anthrax in the air. With luck, we should be able to do that and leave the ship without detection. More important, we would have the information we need to determine if that ship is the threat we think it is. Ma'am, it's worth the risk to find out."

General Darwin replied, "I agree. Do it." but she noticed Alia's body tense ever so slightly as her glance went to Arydin.

The general knew she might be signing these two men's death warrants but she knew they had to make sure they did not blow the wrong ship out of the water. She also had to make sure that ship carried the Anthrax. Hopefully Norm or Arydin would give her that answer.

Chapter 29

General Darwin could not think of any flaws in the plan Norm had briefed her on. Finally, she said, "And, Norm, I expect both Arydin and you back in the command post when that ship is destroyed. Is that clear?"

"Yes, Ma'am," was all Norm could say but he understood the underlying message. Don't screw up and come back safe and sound.

"When do you plan on destroying that ship?" she asked.

"On your orders, Ma'am," he replied.

"Very well. Now for the bad news." and she told them of the phone call she had received from Ehson.

At first none of them knew what to say nor did she give them a chance to comment.

"We have been on the defense far too long. It's time for us to go on the offense if for no other reason than to throw these people off guard and possibly disrupt their plans. And maybe, just maybe we can bring this crisis to an end.

"First, we now know more terrorist involved in this plot will be arriving on both the East and West Coasts within the next forty-eight hours. What we don't know is how they are going to accomplish that.

"To reach either of our coasts, they're going to have to come by air, boat or underwater but which one is the question. We can eliminate one of those avenues simply by closing all air traffic into the United States and I intend to do that by 8 a.m. tomorrow.

"Alia, I want your people to put their thinking caps on and see if they can find any loopholes in our plans. But more important I want you to contact the Navy and put their underwater sonar equipment on full alert around the East and West Coasts and under your full command. I don't want a ship, submarine or large fish coming close to our shores without us knowing it. If you run into any problems with the Navy, call me."

"Yes, Ma'am," was her only reply.

"Norm, can you accomplish your mission and report your findings to me by 5 a.m. tomorrow morning?"

"As you request, Ma'am, it will be done. We may not be back to the command post by then but we will relay our findings to Alia and she will contact you no later than 5 a.m. tomorrow morning."

"Very well. If that ship is our target, I want it blown out of the water at 6 a.m.

"Now, Mr. Protelly, here is what I want you to do. Some of the information I am going to give you I'm sure you already know since it came directly from the FBI's database in Washington, D.C.

"At present there are over three thousand mosques currently established in the United States. On the West Coast, Oregon has twenty, Washington State forty-six, Arizona thirty-seven, New Mexico fourteen and California has six hundred-forty. In California alone, the FBI has had over one hundred of them under surveillance for one reason or another for several years but they have never been able to prove any wrongdoing.

"At the end of this conference I will be sending you a list of those one hundred mosques and their locations. At exactly 5:30 a.m. tomorrow morning I want your agents to arrest every man, woman and child over the age of fifteen at those Mosques. You will coordinate those raids with the military forces I will be assigning to you and they will be providing the transportation needs to move them to holding areas.

"Once there, your people will start screening them. For any reason an individual does not have the proper identification, move them to a separate holding area for further interrogation. Release the ones' cleared immediately and transport them back to the mosque where they came from. Within the next forty-eight hours this threat hopefully will be over. At that time, release those still in confinement. Do you have the agents to accomplish this task or do you need more manpower? If so, I can assign more military personnel to assist you."

"No, General. I have the resources needed to accomplish this but I have two questions. What is the goal for doing this and is it legal?"

"Yes, it will be legal, because at 5 a.m. tomorrow morning, the president will declare Martial Law which will provide you, or the rest of your group, any military assets you need to accomplish your missions and the House and Senate will have approved the president's request.

"I hope this action will disrupt or deter any threat the terrorists may have planned for us. By this time tomorrow, they will know we are onto them and it is they who will be on the defensive. Are there any other questions?"

"Just one," Alia replied, "my group at CIA just asked if we have considered the possibility that this new group of terrorists may have already landed north or south of our coastal borders in either Canada or Mexico and plan on entering the country that way?"

General Darwin sat for a minute or so before she replied, "A point well taken, Alia. Thank your group for me. Also, did they have any recommendations on how to possibly counter that threat?"

"Yes, Ma'am, they did."

"Let's hear it."

"If they have come in on our East Coast, there is a 98 percent probability that they would attempt to enter our country at Quebec or Montreal. That would bring them close to New York. Philadelphia, Baltimore or Washington, D.C. If they should cross on the North-West Coast in British Columbia, there is also a 98 percent probability at Vancouver which would put them close to Seattle, Washington. If they should come in our South-West border there is a 95 percent probability, they would enter at Mexicali which is just south of San Diego."

"And your groups recommendation, Alia?"

"Yes, Ma'am. Place our military personnel at those crossing locations and request Canada and Mexico to do the same."

"Very well, it will be done. If there are no other questions, let's get to work. Be safe and God speed."

Chapter 30

General Darwin took her seat and looked at the people she had just briefed on the action taken place in the country over the past seven days. At the long table situated in the White House bunker, included all the chief of staffs of the Army, Navy, Air Force, Marines and the U.S. Coast Guard, also along with the Senate House majority leaders and Congressman Frank Wolk. The man she watched most closely was President Baker and members of his cabinet who sat at the other end of the table and it was to him she directed her next question.

"Mr. President, you and your staff along with the House, Senate and military Armed Forces are now fully aware of the threat this nation faces. If we are to have any chance in eliminating this threat before they can accomplish their mission to destroy us, we need to act now. Do you have any questions?"

Much to her surprise, the president rose from his seat as if to say something and then fell to the floor.

A few minutes later, the president's physician declared President Baker dead of an apparent massive heart attack.

The room erupted into an uproar and Wendy rose and slapped her hand on the table and in an authoritative voice said, "Sit down." Everyone obeyed that command.

She turned to the secret service agent standing by the door, "Take the president's body out of here now."

After the removal of his body, she turned her attention back to the group. "I'm sorry people but what just happened has only delayed and complicated the issue at hand. We can and will grieve for President Baker later. Right now, we don't have the time, as cold-hearted as that may sound.

"Now where is Vice President Dickson?"

Ed Mason answered, "General, the president directed the vice president be moved yesterday. He is at a secure location, several hundred miles from here. This action was taken as a precaution in case something should happen to him." What he didn't say was it was his request that the president take that action and President Baker had done so reluctantly.

"I should add that the vice president has not been briefed on any of the issues relating to this threat."

Wendy was not surprised that the vice president was not aware of actions taking place in the country. President Baker to her knowledge had never even invited the vice president to the White House since his election let alone brief him on any actions he had taken on government issues. She also knew the vice president was in his early seventies and not in the best of health. What concerned her the most was how he would react to the situation they faced.

Her thoughts were interrupted when she heard Congressman Wolk say, "We do not have time for this. It will take several hours to bring him back here and then brief him on what's going on plus most of us know he is not in good health. Hell, the information he is going to receive could just as easily bring on medical problems we cannot foresee."

"I agree," Wendy stated, "but we have a Constitution that lays out the succession to the presidency and I for one am not going to try and replace it."

"I know, General Darwin, but if the vice president is not available to perform his duties as president, as is the case now, the Constitution clearly states the next in line for the presidency is the Speaker of the House and he's sitting right here. Why can't we swear him in as acting president until the vice president arrives? By then hopefully this crisis will be over."

"Now wait a minute," Senator Stills cried as he rose from his chair. "I am not sure what you're requesting is even legal and I will tell you right now, I don't want to be president even if it's only acting."

"I can sympathize," Congressman Wolk replied "but Senator Stills you are here and we need action now, not hours or days from now, but right this minute. To wait could cost the lives of millions of our citizens."

No one said a word as the conversation unfolded. The Senator raised his hands. "Alright, if everyone in this room agrees. I will do it but I have one condition. As acting president, I want General Darwin to assume complete control of our government and take all actions necessary to win this war against the terrorists. She may not be the president but she is going to act like one. Do you all Agree?"

The raising of hands was unanimous.

Chapter 31

It was almost 3 a.m. when Norm and Arydin surfaced a few hundred feet from the ship. They were not alone. Ten members of Seal Team 7 slowly circled them. Just prior to entering the underwater sleds, provided by the seals, Norm had gone over the plan of actions with each member of the group and ensured they were fully aware of the tasks they were responsible for completing.

When he had originally briefed the men on their tasks and what he and Arydin would be doing, there were objections from several of the Navy Seals. They felt it would be better if they went aboard the ship. Norm was not surprised at the request. In fact, he would have been surprised if they had not voiced their concern.

He had told them he appreciated their request but Arydin and he would be the ones boarding the ship.

"Very well," one of them responded. "How are you going to get on that ship?"

Arydin spoke up, "We really don't have much of a choice. The crew has pulled up the gangway ladder on the side of the ship so the anchor chain is the only avenue."

Another seal asked, "Won't that be the one area they'll be watching the most closely?"

"That's probably true," Arydin replied, "but we know that one individual checks the railings every twenty minutes or so and if they stay on schedule, we will go up the chain anchor right after his inspection. That should give Norm and I plenty of time to get on deck before he or she comes back."

The seal commander now spoke up, "Well gentlemen, there is another way if you wish to try it." He turned and reached into a locker and pulled out what looked like large light-blue rubber gloves. "These were invented by our people and work quite well if you know how to use them. They fit on your hands and feet and they're covered with special suction cups that cling to any surface. My people can train you in a few minutes on their use and you can climb on that ship in any area you wish."

Norm thought to himself, I wish we had more time to see what else they've got that might help in accomplishing this mission but time was not on their side. Within twenty minutes both Arydin and Norm had a set of the gloves and knew how to use them.

As the Navy Seals began the task of planting the mines to the hull of the ship, Norm and Arydin had already reached the deck and were moving toward the tarps. Norm pointed to one tarp on his left and Arydin moved silently in that direction.

Neither man could see any movement on the deck but neither were taking any chances, as they slowly reached the tarps. Norm cut the ropes that secured the tarp and moved inside. Redoing the ties behind him, he turned on the small pencil flash light and saw the hidden items underneath.

The oxygen canisters lay in neat rows secure inside small crates so they could not roll around. This was not proof enough of anything to Norm. There could be any number of reasons the ship was transporting this type of cargo.

Turning off his light, he crawled out from under the tarp and started to move toward the one Arydin was located at when he heard the sound but by then it was too late. Something hit him and his body slammed to the deck, knocking his breath out of him.

He thought he was a dead man when he saw the knife in the man's raised hand, ready to stab him. Without sound, he watched as a figure rose behind the man and he crumbled to the deck with his neck broken.

"Norm, are you OK?" Arydin whispered.

"Yes, thanks to you buddy. I never heard or saw him coming and if you had not shown up when you did, I would probably be dead."

"Well, Norm, as much as I would like to take credit, I think you need to thank the two Navy Seals standing behind you. As I understand it, the seal commander decided it would be best if we had a couple of body guards. They have been with us since we climbed on deck."

Norm thought, so much for being in charge and he turned to see the two men who had saved his life. Neither man was looking in his direction. They were busy surveying the deck of the ship to insure no more visitors suddenly showed up.

Norm just shook his head and turned back to Arydin., "Did you find anything?"

"Yes, and I believe it's what we're looking for. The tarp I looked under is covering many large balloons and small plastic canisters."

"Well, that fits with what I found," Norm stated. "The tarp next to us is covering large oxygen canisters. That tells us they have the capability to inflate those balloons and by hooking the canisters to them they will have the ability to use the wind to carry the Anthrax to the coast. Radio Alia on what we found. I need to dispose of the body. It may give us a little more time. If they find the body, they will know for sure that we're onto them. I'll push him overboard and maybe they will think he fell overboard or deserted."

As Norm reached for the body the two Navy Seals pulled the man to the deck railing and slid him overboard then waited for Norm and Arydin to leave the ship. Only then did they follow them.

At exactly 6 a.m., the ship blew up in a huge ball of flame and sunk to the bottom of the ocean without the requirement of the Navy submarine. The Navy Seals had done their job well. The ship had sunk within two minutes of exploding but Norm was taking no chances. He ordered the sub to surface and check to see if there were any survivors. There were none.

Chapter 32

General Darwin sat in the White House bunker watching the actions taking place across the United States on the large wall maps. And the situation board spelled out the actions already taken place or were ongoing in real-time.

Norm and his people had taken out the ship on the West Coast before it could do any harm. She had the Federal Aviation Administration (FAA) close all the airspace both on the East and West Coasts and the FBI had accomplished its mission on removing the people from the one hundred mosques. Of the several thousand-people detained, they relocated only seventy-three individuals to other places for further interrogation. They arrested only seventeen individuals and their status would be determined later. Right now, they were not a threat and would remain so until this was over.

Alia's warning of a possible attack from land at the northern and southern coasts was another matter. The terrorist had indeed attempted crossing from Canada and Mexico into the United States. What had surprised her was the number of terrorists involved. At least fifty had attempted the northern crossings and twenty on the southern border. In the battles that ensued, all the terrorists had died.

The fifty terrorists who attempted to enter the country through Montreal, Canada made the mistake of coming in as one group. At 8:15 a.m., they entered the local train station and attempted to board a train bound for Washington, D.C. They even had fake boarding passes. To blend in with the other passengers, some dressed in business suits but the majority wore jeans and carried backpacks.

They did not know that a reception committee was waiting for them. The Canadian government was aware of the threat to the U.S., thanks to General Darwin, and they were taking no chances that they might be part of it too.

Canadian Military Special Forces and other security forces had deployed to the suspected areas including all the train stations. Most of the security teams hid from the public in holding areas ready to respond at a moment's notice.

It didn't take long. As the terrorist started boarding the train one of them stumbled and fell on the platform floor and an AK-47 fell from his knapsack. That's all it took and the battle was on but it was a blood bath for both sides.

The terrorist shot at anything that moved and some that did not. It was over in less than twenty minutes but some three hundred-fifty people were dead or injured.

All the terrorist fought until they died and took as many people as they could with them. It didn't make any difference to them if it was men, women or children but in the long run General Darwin knew it had been a victory for Canada and the United States.

The Canadian government had found more than a dozen canisters in some of the backpacks and thought they contained Anthrax. General Darwin thought so too and ordered them sent to Edgewood Arsenal but there was no doubt in her mind on what was in those canisters.

The terrorist who entered from Mexicali, Mexico was a different matter. They also started their penetration into the United States at 8 a.m. but instead of as a group they came through the border crossing in five vans a few minutes apart and turned on to I-8 heading west to San Diego, some twenty-five miles away.

The border crossing was normally busy at this time of the morning but on this day every vehicle stopped and driver's license checked before allowed to go through. The stop took no more than a few minutes.

The drivers were not aware of hidden camera's transmitting images of each driver, their driver's license and license plate to a motor vehicle database in Washington, D.C. Within minutes, the five vehicles were identified and the second part of the trap was waiting for them.

Some twenty miles away, State police shut down I-8 west due to what appeared to be a major car accident. All traffic came to a complete stop but within minutes it appeared that the state police had set up a detour moving traffic across the interstate away from the accident site. When the terrorist in the first van approached the turnaround, they realized it was a trap. They opened fire on the police and attempted to crash through the barricade but to no avail as other vehicles suddenly blocked their way.

Within seconds the men in the van were dead as Army Rangers poured out of the supposedly wrecked vehicles and other hidden places alongside of the road. It only took a few minutes and the terrorist in the other vehicles were dead as well.

Upon inspection of the five vans the terrorists were driving, they found that each held several gas masks and a large canister bolted to the floor. The canisters had a hose attached to a pipe that led under the floorboard and out the back of the van.

The general was now aware of how they intended to attack San Diego. All they would have to do was drive around any high place, such as an overpass or bridge in the city, and release the Anthrax into the air and no one would have noticed.

The terrorists had planned well and all she could think was thank God they failed.

Chapter 33

Norm and his group sat watching on the large screen as General Darwin briefed the government and military officials in the White House bunker on the actions taken and the outcome of each terrorist attack within the country.

Then she stated, "Whoever was responsible for this attack on our country spent an enormous amount of time, money and planning to make sure it was a success. We are very lucky they failed. If they had accomplished their mission thousands if not millions of our people could have died.

"The reason they did not was partly luck and the dedication of a few of our people who made sure we were able to track them down before they could do our country any harm. They are the heroes who deserve the recognition for saving our country and soon every American will know their names. But first we must determine who was responsible for the attack and more important what we are going to do about it."

"General Darwin, do we have any idea who would attempt to do such a cowardly act?" Congressman Wolk asked.

"We are working on it," the general replied. "At present all of our intelligence agencies are trying to find that answer and I have no doubt that we will have that answered within the next few days." What she did not say was that she already felt she knew the answer.

Before she could continue the large screen went blank and then she saw the image of Alia appear.

"General, we need to talk now." And the screen again went blank.

Chapter 34

General Darwin did not hesitate. She asked everyone in the room to keep their seats then she walked into the next room where the White House Communications Agency was located. She took a seat in front of a computer and said, patch me in please. That was all it took and she could see Alia and the rest of Norm's group.

"All right, Alia. "What's the problem.?"

"General, as you directed, I put all the Navy's underwater sonar systems on the East and West Coasts on full alert yesterday. As you know those sonar systems have been placed close to our borders. To be exact some two hundred miles out but we do have some as far away as five hundred miles. A few minutes ago, my team at CIA who have been monitoring the system along with the Navy advised me that there appears to be several blips at the outer edge of our warning systems on both coasts and they're moving toward our shores."

"What does the Navy say?" The general asked.

"They believe they're miniature submarines," Alia answered. "At the speed they are traveling they should be within two hundred miles of our coasts within the next forty-eight hours."

"Very well, Alia. I will have the Navy take care of this threat."

Before she could continue Alia interrupted her. "General, I think we found how the terrorists have been directing this attack against our county."

"How?" General Darwin asked.

"Well, ever since all this started, I have had NASA looking for any signals that may have been going on between the various groups who have attacked us. It now appears that all the communications going on through the groups seem to be coming from a single source. I believe that source is the mastermind directing this attack. It seems all the communications between the various terrorist groups are coming from that single location."

"Can you tell me where that location is, Alia?"

"Yes, Ma'am, I can. The signal appears to be coming from the state of Nebraska. This is the central part of the country so it's logical that they would locate there."

"Where in Nebraska?" the general asked.

"The signals have been traced close to the small town of Brewster, Nebraska. And, General, FBI records indicate a mosque was built close to that location several years ago. The FBI believe that there are approximately two hundred people located there."

The general looked at the group for a few seconds and then said, "Very well. I will have the Navy take care of the sub threat. Norm, you Arydin and Protelly, along with any military assets you feel you may need, will eliminate the threat that mosque is to our county. You have less than twenty-four hours to complete it." Before Norm could reply the screen went blank.

Nick Protelly was the first to speak, "She doesn't ask for much, does she?"

"No," Norm replied, "and we had better get with it."

Chapter 35

Some twenty hours later, Norm and his group along with some fifty FBI agents and fifty Army Ranger personnel were in the large Bessy Recreational Complex located in the Nebraska National Forest some seven miles from the mosque near the town of Brewster, Nebraska.

When Norm had found out the town of Brewster had a population of only three hundred fifty souls, he knew it would not be wise to bring any of his people into the area. The local population, including people from the mosque, would notice any outsiders. A chance he was not willing to take. So, under the cover of darkness, he had a group of Rangers bring a tent into the area and camouflage it. Even from a short distance, it was hidden from view.

"All right people, let's go over it one more time," Norm said.

And Alia started the briefing. "As you are all aware, the Navy destroyed all twenty-four miniature subs trying to get close to our shores. That's the good news. The bad news is that the people located in the mosque probably know it as well and may be on alert for an attack there. I hope not but we need to be prepared for such an event.

"We also know there are some two hundred people living at the mosque. We have determined that there are no children with that group and only a few women so that means we may be up against two hundred terrorists that will probably fight to the death, if discovered. Let's hope that is not the case because our planning is based on a surprise attack and we have a smaller force. If they are not waiting for us that should be enough. If they are, then we're outnumbered by almost two-to-one. Between the fifty FBI agents and the fifty Army Rangers we have one hundred personnel to do the job. Surprise should give us the edge we need.

"If it does not work out that way our backup plan will go into effect. I presently have three drones circling the area and as a last resort those drones will destroy the mosque and anyone in it or close by. That would include any of our people as well. Let's hope it does not come to that." And she looked at Arydin then turned away.

"Each of you have a copy of the construction plans that were used to build the mosque some seven years ago. This three-story complex is a well-designed and constructed building to provide protection for the people residing there. The eight-foot wall around the complex should not be a problem for our people but the five-story narrow tower, located at the far corner of the complex used to call people to prayers, is another matter. It's guarded twenty-four hours a day by four individuals. And I can assure you they are not there to call people to prayers. Our Rangers have been tasked to eliminate that threat so no alarm is called before we strike."

Norm stood and looked at the group. "It's now 2 a.m. That gives us two and one-half hours to get our people in place. At 4:30 a.m. we will attack."

Norm turned to Protelly, "If it's all right with you, Arydin and I will go with you."

"I wouldn't have it any other way," Nick replied, "so let's get on with it."

At exactly 4:30 a.m., they stormed the mosque and the surprise was complete. The fighting had been close and vicious but it was over within thirty minutes. Alia had been right; all the terrorist had fought until they died.

At 6 a.m., Norm called General Darwin and briefed her on the results of the attack.

The mosque had been the nerve center for the planned attack on the U.S. They found all the evidence needed in the underground command post and communications center. They had also found a large amount of Anthrax, which Norm had put under guard until personnel from Edgewood Arsenal could arrive to remove it.

Finally, General Darwin asked, "And our causalities?"

In a somber voice Norm replied, "Out of one hundred three personnel who stormed the building, fourteen were killed and twenty-six were injured. Almost 40 percent of our people were casualties, either injured or dead. We lost Nick Protelly who died protecting Arydin who's condition is serious but he's alive. He along with most of the injured have been airlifted to a hospital at Omaha, Nebraska."

"And you, Norm?" she asked.

"I'm OK, Ma'am," he replied.

"Don't give me that crap, Norm. I asked how you are."

"It could have been worse. I took two hits but none of the injuries are life-threating. The medics patched me up and I'm just one of the walking wounded. I will be fine, General Darwin."

"And Arydin?" she asked.

"Not very good I'm afraid."

The general could hear the anguish in his voice as he continued.

He took two bullets to his chest and the medics did not hold out much chance for his recovery. I sent Alia with him to Omaha."

"Thank you, Norm. The country owes you a great debt." She paused for a second and then said, "Your father would have been proud of you." And the connection ended.

General Darwin sat staring at the phone for the longest few second then reached for it. It was a phone number she had never used before and when Ehson answered all she said was, "The time is near and we need to meet right away."

Ehson replied, "Very well. I am on my way." and the phone line went dead. It was 6:55 a.m.

At 12 noon, Eastern Standard Time, the city of Carush ceased to exist and the mushroom cloud rose high into the sky.

Chapter 36

Over five years had passed since the unsuccessful attack on the country and Wendy was once again visiting Arlington National Cemetery. She saw the solitary military guard come to attention and salute her, as she neared the gravesite. She returned it then looked down on the headstones and felt the warmth course through her.

Norm Shepard and Arydin Hassan in full military uniforms stood behind her along with Alia. Both men had a Medal of Honor draped around their dress uniforms.

She became aware of the small hand that clasped hers and the little girl about four years old asked, "Who were these people?"

Wendy knelt beside her god-daughter until they were at eye level. She thought to herself, she looks just like her mother, Alia, but she could also see Arydin there as well.

"Just some very old friends, Farah, just some old friends," and she rose to leave then stopped and turned to the guard.

"Master Sergeant Dotson, thank you for your service."

"It is my honor, Madam President," and he watched until they left the area.

###

Don't miss out!

Visit the website below and you can sign up to receive emails whenever Ray Derby publishes a new book. There's no charge and no obligation.

https://books2read.com/r/B-A-MPMDB-ZNUVC

BOOKS 2 READ

Connecting independent readers to independent writers.

Did you love *Cold Wind*? Then you should read *Heavy Silence*[1] by Ray Derby!

It was a job he did not want but when an unknown number of people had detonated a nuclear weapon in the Pacific Ocean, he was quickly appointed by several of the nuclear powers to find out who actually was responsible and why.

It did not take long for Brad and his small team to determine a large group of Muslims had been working for years to rule the world and now two million Muslim terrorists were ready to accomplish their mission.

What the terrorists did not know, or for that matter very few people in the world knew, Brad Dyer had one occupation and that was to destroy any terrorist group he became involved with. To his enemies he was called "The Cobra."

Read more at www.rayderby.com.

---

1. https://books2read.com/u/bwVrry

2. https://books2read.com/u/bwVrry

About the Author

I was born in Sioux City, Iowa. After graduating from school, I joined the U.S. Navy. That started my career of traveling all over the world. Just before my enlistment was up, I flew around the world in seven days. On returning to Sioux City, I married, raised four children and began a career in emergency management.

I started as a volunteer emergency civil defense worker, then a full-time civil defense director, and a civilian disaster preparedness officer for the U.S. Air Force. For 26 years before my retirement, I was a federal emergency coordinator for several federal agencies.

Over the years, many people have asked why I chose this profession, and I always give the same answer. If I could save one life, all of it would be worth it. What I did not say was that I was out to save thousands of lives if a major disaster should occur. I have never regretted the path I chose. It was a remarkable career that led me right to the steps of the White House.

Read more at www.rayderby.com.

www.ingramcontent.com/pod-product-compliance
Lightning Source LLC
Chambersburg PA
CBHW052141170626
46812CB00004B/1531